Ian R McCourt was born in Manchester in 1945. He has been married to Angela for 27 years and has a daughter, Sara, and a son, Grant, who, together with his four granddaughters are the loves of his life.

He has led an exceptionally full and somewhat chequered life, but now likes to do nothing more than to write, or sit fishing on the river bank facing his home, pondering why most of the fish get away.

CLINK

Ian R McCourt

CLINK

Vanguard Press

VANGUARD PAPERBACK

© Copyright 2009
Ian R McCourt

The right of Ian R McCourt to be identified as author of
this work has been asserted by him in accordance with the
Copyright, Designs and Patents Act 1988.

All Rights Reserved

No reproduction, copy or transmission of this publication
may be made without written permission.
No paragraph of this publication may be reproduced,
copied or transmitted save with the written permission of the publisher,
or in accordance with the provisions
of the Copyright Act 1956 (as amended).

Any person who commits any unauthorised act in relation to
this publication may be liable to criminal
prosecution and civil claims for damages.

A CIP catalogue record for this title is
available from the British Library.

ISBN 978 1 84386 495 0

Vanguard Press is an imprint of
Pegasus Elliot MacKenzie Publishers Ltd.
www.pegasuspublishers.com

First Published in 2009

Vanguard Press
Sheraton House Castle Park
Cambridge England

Printed & Bound in Great Britain

ACKNOWLEDGEMENTS

To my wife Angela, my daughter Sara and son Grant for all their support in the past and the truth kept a secret for so many years, and the continued support in the writing of this book.

AUTHOR'S NOTE

This is a true story, but due to the contents, names of people and places have been changed. It may seem a great deal of the contents suggest a prison term is one of fun and games; only people who have unfortunately experienced a term of imprisonment would agree that this is far from the case. Many of the pranks played may appear to be acts of irresponsible people bent on self-destruction but this is far from the truth; it is the act of self-survival in a world where all your loved ones are away from you and always knowing that you are the cause of the suffering that they are undergoing due to your mistakes.

It is about men, who for various reasons, some of them for serious and some of them not so serious crimes, create a bond that will never be forgotten. The reader may consider that the men portrayed in the book did not care and treated the system as some kind of joke. This again is not the truth for the majority of them – many of the games played were games men played when they were at their lowest ebb. I ask those who do so to look at their lives and ask themselves how close have they come. John Davidson did a stupid thing, but may I add without the knowledge it was a serious crime, however it still was a crime, but never to be repeated.

I hope the readers enjoy the humour, but can also look deeper into why some of the acts were done, which enabled these men to stay sane.

Chapter 1

"We will be landing in approximately 10 minutes. Could you please make sure that your seat belts are fastened and your seat is in an upright position."

"Well that's it for another year," John said, to Amy as they prepared to get back to reality after a two weeks' holiday in Greece. The two children Emma who was six and Carl who was three had a great time. John was sure over the past months they had felt the strain; they had saved hard for this holiday after a disastrous year of John having lost his job and them having to move into John's mother's house in Manchester, but were looking forward to moving into their new house and John's continued success in the new job he had started three weeks before their holiday.

The plane arrived on time and having cleared Customs without any problems, not that they had anything that they had to declare, they made their way to the rank for a taxi to Bristol railway station.

The train arrived on time at Manchester and within half an hour they were on the doorstep of John's mother's.

The door opened to be confronted by Dorothy, John's mother with a somewhat sombre greeting, which immediately told John and Amy that something was wrong.

"Hi Mum, nice to be back," John said with a somewhat watery smile on his face anticipating a problem had arisen while they had been away.

"Nice to see you back, have you had a good time?"

"Great," both said simultaneously.

"Why don't you take your bags upstairs?" John's mother said to the children. With that the children ran up as requested.

"The police came round yesterday," John's mother said without further ado; she never was one to keep news to herself for long.

"What for?" John said, with a feeling of dread going through him.

"I don't know, they would not tell me but they want to see you at Chester Road Police Station at 10.30 tomorrow."

"Did they say what this was about?" John said.

"Nothing just that it was important that you were there at 10.30, and ask to see D.C. Simons and D.S. Gill from West Midlands Police."

"West Midlands Police?" wondering what a visit from officers 100 miles away would want him for.

"What could it be about?" Amy said, with a rather worried look on her face.

"It can't be much," John replied, racking his brain what he had done. He had always been a 'Jack the Lad' and had done a few shady deals over the years in his job in buying and selling, but he could think of nothing that would warrant the police to visit his mother's house looking for him.

Chapter 2

After a restless night and unable to sleep for long periods worried about what tomorrow would bring, John got up at 7am; watching the clock, the fingers of which went round very slowly, waiting for the time he could go to the police station on Chester Road to find out why they wanted to see him.

The drive took him half an hour and he approached the desk inside the police station with a feeling of trepidation, even though he had no idea what it could be about. "John Davidson," John said to the ruddy-faced constable behind the desk, "I have come to see D.C. Simons and D.S. Gill."

The ruddy-faced constable looked at a large pad of notes and asked John to sit down pointing to a green painted metal chair. After about half an hour a door opened at the back of the reception area and a tall man in an immaculate grey suit came over to John.

"John Davidson?" he asked.

"Yes," John replied, with a slight shake in his voice, he did not know why because he had nothing to hide.

"Come with me if you will please."

John got up from his chair and followed the man through the door and up a flight of stairs into a small office with a desk and three wooden chairs. On one of the chairs was another tall man and again dressed in a grey suit. As John approached he stood up and introduced himself as Detective Sergeant Gill and introduced the man who had escorted him from the reception area as Detective Constable Simons.

"Sit down will you please," said the D.C.

"What is this about?" said John, feeling that he had to say something even though he knew he would soon find out.

The D.C. held his hand out to his colleague who handed him a red file with some writing on that John could not read. The D.C. sat down and started to take papers out of the folder. John noticed there were rather a considerable amount of them.

"John we are from the West Midlands and we have come up to ask you a few questions regarding your purchase two years ago, July 1980 to be exact, of a house in Crown Road Birmingham."

John's mind went back to that time and the time he had met Dave Cross in the Duck Pub in the centre of Birmingham. He had not seen Dave for some years, having been a drinking pal up North.

Chapter 3

"What the hell are you doing in Brum?" said John, pleased to see his old drinking buddy.

"Hi John, nice to see you. I moved about three months ago to take a job down here, and bought a new house on Crown Road. Best buy I have ever had. What are you up to now?"

"Still in buying and selling."

"Oh and how's Amy and the kids?"

"Well," John replied, "to answer the first question, yes, still earning a buck, and to the second question, I'm afraid that Amy and I split up last year. We're are still in touch with each other but that is all."

"Sorry to hear that," said Dave, with a genuine look of surprise on his face.

"Well, that's the way things go," said John. "Anyway let's have a drink. What is it buddy? Still on drop dead strong lager?"

"Yep," said Dave, as he finished the last drop in his glass. They sat down and the question of houses came up with Dave telling John about the new house he had bought on Crown Road. He said it was a new estate of detached three bedrooms, lounge, nice kitchen and gardens at a crazy price of £40,000.

"Bloody hell!" John said. "That's cheap."

"Sure is," said Dave. "The only thing is it's in a red light area and you tend to get rather a lot of trouble at night when the pro's and pimps are about, not to mention the kerb crawlers, but at that price I intend to sell it next year and make a good few bob on it. After all, the girls and their pimps have to have somewhere to live."

"Bloody hell!" John said. "I wouldn't have minded a bit of that action myself now I am on my own, and renting a house in Northfield. I could put up with that crap for a year or so and, let's face it, if you get lonely all you have to do is knock on the window."

"Never change do you? No wonder Amy gave you the heave ho, but if you are serious, I have a good mate in the mortgage game and I think there are still one or two up for sale. Why not come round tomorrow and have a look at mine?"

"Why not?" John said. "Nothing to lose." They finished their drinks and arranged for John to see Dave the following day.

"Christ these aren't bad. Pity about the area – I see what you mean, bit grotty to say the least but to make a few bob in a year or so I think I could put up with it. The only thing is I don't have any spare money to put down as deposit."

"Don't worry," Dave said, "neither did I. You know the guy I told you about last night? He can sort it out for you, it may cost you a drink but he sorted it out for me without any deposit no problems. Tell you what, let me give him a ring and see what he says."

"OK, why not," John said, "ask him if we could meet him for a beer in the Duck at lunchtime today."

Dave went in the kitchen and came back after a few minutes sporting a large smile. "Sorted, one to half past today."

"This is John, John this is Frank." They sat down at a table in the corner of the lounge bar where they could talk without being overheard and Frank went through all the details of securing a mortgage with no deposit for the house on Crown Road.

After about an hour and three pints later, Frank looked at John and said, "Well mate that is about it, what do you think?" John sat there looking into his half empty glass for a few moments quickly working out the repayment side of things, which he had done since the short meeting with Frank and decided he could not go wrong. "OK," said John. "How much?"

"What do you mean?" said Frank.

"I mean how much is this going to cost me up front?"

"Two hundred pounds arrangement fee up front and that is it," Frank said with a smile on his face. "And I will do the rest. I will sort all the paperwork out within the next seven days and give you a ring when we can meet back here and put pen to paper if you are still happy."

John looked at Dave who had said very little during the past hour apart from asking what we wanted to drink. "Sounds good," he said to Dave.

"Worked well for me," Dave replied. He turned back to Frank, looked him in the eye for any signs of untruth, seeing none held out his hand to him and said, "GO FOR IT."

During the next week John carried on as usual meeting up with Dave for a few drinks in the Duck awaiting the call from Frank. Friday arrived and John was sitting at home when the phone rang, it was Frank. "Hi Frank."

"All sorted. Have got all the papers for your signature. I take it you are still up for it John?"

"Sure am," John said. "When can we meet up?"

"How about tomorrow lunch in the Duck?" Frank replied.

"Sounds good to me," John said. "I'll give Dave a bell and we can have a celebration drink. See you tomorrow about twelve."

The following day as arranged the three of them sat in the Duck with three pints in front of them and the all important papers on the table.

"Have you brought the two hundred with you?" Frank said to John.

"Sure have, got it in cash, thought that it would be better for you."

"Sure is," Frank said, and with that John handed a brown envelope over to him. "Better count it," he said.

"I'm sure it will be OK," said Frank as he put the envelope in his inside jacket pocket and took a pen out of the same pocket and put it down on top of the papers on the table. "Right all I need is your autograph here, and here," as he pointed to the papers. "I have arranged for Clive Wright, a solicitor friend of mine, to contact you regarding the legal side of things."

"OK, fine," said John. "When do you expect everything to be completed as I have to terminate my rental agreement on my house I am in at the moment?"

"You should be able to move in within the month I would expect," Frank said.

John left them at the pub and went home to write to his landlord giving him one month's notice, which he did not get round to doing.

All went well during the next three weeks. John went from strength to strength in his business and was earning bundles, then out of the blue one night the telephone rang and it was Amy. "Hi how are you?" she said.

"Good," John said, not really feeling good. In spite of the purchase of his new house he was becoming increasingly lonely and missed the kids like hell. "How's things?" John said thinking how nice it was to hear her voice.

"Well to tell you the truth I have been doing a lot of thinking the past few weeks and I think we should have a talk."

"About what?" John said.

"Well in spite of you having been a total bastard with your playing around, deep down I still love you, and the children and I miss you like hell."

John was taken aback to say the least. He had thought that Amy and the children were lost forever after his last of many affairs had been found out yet again, which had resulted in Amy leaving and going back to her parents in Dorset. "I too have missed you like hell," John said. "What shall we do? I didn't think you would miss me after all I had put you through."

"Let's talk," she said. John's heart jumped. He never thought he would hear those words from Amy in a million years. "God yes," he said, "When?"

"Why not come down to Dorset next week and see what happens? But before you do there are strict conditions and I mean strict."

"OK," John said. "I will give you a ring tomorrow and sort something out."

"OK," she said. "Look forward to speaking to you later, but remember strict conditions. Oh and I do still love you, bye."

John could not believe that he still may have a chance with his family. He had given up hope a long time ago and now, WOW! It seemed that he might stand a chance of being back with Amy and the children.

Time, what time is it he thought? He looked at the clock on the wall that told him it was five thirty, four maybe five hours to Dorset. NO John thought to himself, you can't do it now, can you? He thought, like fuck I can. Before he knew what he was doing, he was on the motorway down to Dorset.

Half past nine he was outside a phone box near Amy's parents' home. She will think I'm nuts he thought, nevertheless before he could think any further he was dialling Amy's parents' phone. "Hello," the voice on the other end said. He immediately recognised it as Amy's. "Hi, it's me."

"Hi, didn't expect a call so quick," Amy said.

"Just thought I would give you a ring to see if you fancied a drink tonight," John said.

"TONIGHT? You're in Birmingham how could we have a drink tonight?"

"Wrong. I can see your front door, I've just driven down." There was a silence from the other end of the phone.

"You are joking?" Amy said.

"No I'm serious, see you in one minute," and with that put the phone down afraid of any rejection. The door was open and Amy was stood on the doorstep by the time he got there. John wanted to take her in his arms, but didn't know what to do, or how to act. That problem was soon sorted out as Amy rushed to him and put her arms around him. John responded by holding her close to him saying nothing but feeling ecstatic that he was once more in the arms of his wife. They went in the lounge to be confronted by Amy's mother and father, who to John's surprise seemed glad to see him. He went over to Amy's mother and gave her a kiss on the cheek and shook her father's hand. "Nice to see you," John said.

"And you," they both said together. "The children are in bed," her mother said.

"That's OK," John said, feeling a little uneasy.

Amy broke the expected silence and said, "Well what about this drink you want to take me for?"

"OK let's go," John said. Wishing Amy's mother and father goodbye, they left the house and went over to John's car and drove to the local hotel bar and found a seat near the window. He went to the bar not having to ask Amy what she wanted to drink assuming she still had a dry white wine. He returned with the drinks and sat facing Amy, not quite sure how to start the conversation.

It was Amy who saved him by starting, "Well," she said, "what are we to do about our situation? I love you and want to be with you, but I can't the way you have behaved over the past years. I can't put up with your playing around. I was young and stupid at first, but I have grown up and a bit more streetwise. Do you or don't you want to have me and the children back as a family?"

John looked at her and realised how much Amy HAD grown up during their twelve months apart, and knew that she was serious and this was his last chance. "Yes I do want us back as a family. I have missed you so much. Please come back with me to Birmingham."

Amy smiled at him but then put on a serious face. "John I will, but I will tell you now that any going back to your old ways and it is over for good, and I mean that, understand?"

"I promise," John said, (and he meant it). He leaned over and gave Amy a kiss with a tear in his eye at the thought of him having another chance with his wife and children.

"I forgot," Amy said, "Where are you going to stay tonight?"

John held his breath for a moment and then said, "Well I have booked a double room in the Bluebell Hotel down the road."

She looked at him with a smile on her face, "A double room?"

"Er yes, I just thought."

"I know what you thought," Amy interjected with an even bigger smile on her face. "Come on, let's get back to mum's to pick a few things up."

Early the following morning they were going through the front door of Amy's parents' house just as the children were getting up. With big smiles on their faces they ran up to John, arms open wide. "Daddy," they both shouted as they launched themselves at him. He held them close for a long time not wanting to ever let them go.

"How would you like to come to your new house with me and mummy?" John asked.

"YES, YES," they both screamed.

An hour later after saying goodbye to Amy's parents and having a brief but stern talk from them both they were back on the motorway up to Birmingham and a new life for them all.

Four hours or so later Amy and the children were inspecting their new house. "It's lovely," Amy said, putting her arms around John. "First thing we will have to do tomorrow is to sort school out."

"One just round the corner," said John still not believing they were together again.

All of a sudden, a terrible thought came into John's head, the bloody house on Crown Road, he had not given it a thought. The past twenty-four hours with all that had been going on, NO way could he take his family to a house in a rough red light area. All the paperwork had been done and contracts signed, what the hell am I going to do? He knew he couldn't tell Amy, she would say that they would move, but John knew he could not subject his family to living in that area.

"What's the matter?" said Amy noticing a change in his mood.

"Nothing," said John, "just that I was going to get a bottle of wine to celebrate. I'll just nip down the road and get one." John jumped into the car with his head spinning and went down the road to the Duck. He had to have a little time to think on his own, and by God he could do with a drink. As he walked into the pub he saw Dave at the bar.

"Hi buddy," Dave said. "How's things?"

"Great and not so great," John said, and after ordering them both a drink started to tell Dave of the last twenty-four hours.

"That's fantastic news," Dave said.

"Sure is," he said, "but for one small matter."

"What's that?" Dave asked.

After taking a long drink of his beer he said, "Crown Road."

"Oh shit," said Dave. "You can't take the kids to live in that area."

"I know, I know," he said, "but what the fuck can I do, everything is sorted."

After a few minutes Dave said, "Let's look at this one step at a time, you know you can't take the family to Crown Road. What has it cost you?"

"Two hundred quid to Frank that's all."

"Forget the bloody place and stay where you are for the time being."

"I can't just forget it," John said, "or can I, after all if I don't move in and nothing is paid off the mortgage they would, I assume, just repossess it."

"Exactly," said Dave.

Feeling a little better now, he said goodbye to Dave and set off for home via the supermarket to buy a bottle of wine.

Chapter 4

Things had gone well during the year. John and Amy were as happy as ever and even managed to save a few thousand pounds. Nothing was heard about Crown Road. Dave had sold his house and had moved back up north to take another job, so he had lost his drinking pal which was not such a bad thing as it stopped him going into the pub as much.

One night John was sitting at home reading the local paper when his eyes moved to the property for sale section. He started to look at the property for sale in the Bourneville area of Birmingham. John had always liked that area as it was close to the city centre but still very rural. His eyes locked in on a property on Lynn Road. He read it out in his mind, semi detached, three bedrooms, lounge, dining room, garage and large well kept gardens, it was just the house and area that he would like if he was looking to buy but he wasn't, or was he? He turned to Amy and said, "Listen to this," and began to read the details out to her.

"Sounds nice," she said. "Are you thinking about having a look at it?"

"Wouldn't mind," John said. "After all we can't stay here for ever and we have saved a few bob and work is stable and going well, no harm in just having a look."

They pulled up outside number 10 Lynn Road and saw the estate agent was already there waiting to show them round. He greeted them just as the front door opened and the present owner stood in the doorway. They spent about half an hour looking at the house and were very impressed by the size and condition and more than anything the price. After saying goodbye to the owner and the agent they decided to go to the Duck for a drink and to talk more about the house.

"Well what did you think?" John said to Amy as they sat down with a drink each.

"Very nice," Amy said, "but can we afford it and what about furniture, remember our house at present is fully furnished. We would have to buy all new furniture, and then there is the deposit?"

"I can sort out the deposit," he said, his mind going back to Frank.

"Well if you are sure," Amy said, "but we have to look at things very carefully. The last thing we want to do is take something on we can't afford."

They finished their drinks and left the pub for home.

John put down the phone, "Well," he said to Amy, "that's that, I have spoken to the estate agent and put in an offer, all we have to do now is wait for them to get back to see if the people who are selling it will accept the offer."

Two hours later the phone rang, it was the estate agent to tell them he had put the offer to the owners and they had accepted it. "Now all we have to do is to sort the mortgage out," John said. "I will get in touch with my man first thing in the morning."

John was once more in the Duck waiting for Frank to turn up, he was half way through his drink when Frank walked in. "Drink?" he said to John.

"Cheers, usual please Frank."

Frank came back from the bar with a drink in each hand and put John's down in front of him.

"Right," he said to John, "what can I do for you?"

John began to tell him about the house on Lynn Road, after he had finished Frank said, "What about the house you purchased last year on Crown Road?" John gave a nervous cough and started to tell Frank all about Amy and the children and not being able to bring himself to move into Crown Road and the fact that he had just let it die a death.

"Wow, that could be a problem getting a mortgage," Frank said.

"What would be the problem?" John said but anticipating the answer.

"Put it this way John, if you put down on the mortgage application form that you had a mortgage that you never paid and the property was repossessed, how do you think the lenders would look at it?"

"Take your point Frank, is there any way round it?"

Frank took a drink from his glass and looked in deep thought. "Well, yes there is but is a bit naughty to say the least. We could put you down as a first time buyer but as I say it's a bit naughty, I have done it a few times without any problems though."

"Well can we do it that way? I don't want to tell Amy we can't get a mortgage due to having had one that I cocked up."

"It's up to you if you want to go down that road, I have the docs in my car we can fill them in now, if you like?"

"What about deposit?" John said.

"I can do it on the same deal as last time, two hundred arrangement fee."

"As was said last time, GO FOR IT."

"For fuck's sake, will you forget last time, there was NO last time." With that he went outside to his car while John went to the bar to get more drinks.

After about half an hour all the paperwork was completed, "Is a cheque for the two hundred, OK?" said John.

"Fine," Frank said, "but can you leave the payee blank?"

John took his cheque book out of his inside pocket and wrote out a cheque and handed it to Frank.

"I'll get one of my pet solicitors to write to you over the next few days and arrange to see you when completion is ready."

"Good, thanks again Frank, want another drink before you go?"

"No thanks," he replied. "Have got someone else to see in half an hour, will be in touch." With that the mortgage man left. John decided to have one more drink and the set off on the ten minute drive home to give Amy the good news.

"All done and dusted," he said to Amy as he walked in the door.

"I take it everything was OK?" she said as she came over and gave him a kiss.

"No problem, just got to wait to hear from the lenders and the solicitors and then it is all go."

It was a good job it was all go, the following morning they received a letter from the landlord's agent saying that the owner of their house was coming home from living abroad and would want the house back for him and his wife to live in and giving them two months' notice.

"Well that saves writing to them," John said with a smile. "Funny thing, fate don't you think?" he said to Amy.

Time went fast and before they knew where they were they had received the offer from the loan company. They had been to the solicitors and signed the completion documents, and purchased most of the furniture they required which just about brought their bank balance to zero.

They were stood in the lounge of their new house waiting for the removal van and delivery from the various stores they had bought the furniture from.

For the next year things went well with John and Amy and they settled into the house well for them both and the children. It was the happiest time they had had since they had been together, they had even booked a two week holiday in Greece. And then it was a downward slope.

It all happened one Friday morning at 10.30 with a telephone call from John's supplier. "John," the voice said on the other end of the phone. "I think you should come into the office, we have a problem, in fact quite a serious problem."

"Like what?" John said, with a feeling of impending doom.

"I will tell you when you come in," the voice said. "See you in about thirty minutes, OK?" With that the line went dead.

John arrived at the office about an hour later and walked into the office to be confronted by the two men he had dealt with for a long time, both looked a bit shaken with a look of total panic on their faces.

"Better sit down," one of the men said as he pointed to a chair.

"Well what's this all about?" John said as he took the chair. He had a dread of the answer; he knew for some reason this was not going to be good.

"Well," said one of the men, "I'm not going to beat around the bush, we are having to close shop."

— Business troubles

"Close shop?" John said. "Why?"

"Problem is, we can't get supplies from abroad anymore, or at least from our main supplier, and it means in a nut shell that is it."

John looked first at one of the men and then the other with total disbelief. "Jesus, when?"

"Now," said one of the men. "I'm sorry John, but there is nothing we can do."

John left the office in a state of shock, wondering what the hell he and Amy were to do; life had been so good, and now it had gone pear shaped in a big way.

He parked the car in his drive and walked to the front door of his house. What the hell am I going to say to Amy, he thought as the door opened to see Amy waiting for him on the doorstep.

"Pour me a drink will you Amy?" he said as he walked into the lounge. Amy could see that something had gone wrong and brought John a large scotch.

John spent the next hour and four more large drinks telling Amy what had gone on in the office, trying to think what their next move would be. It was obvious John had to find another way of bringing money into the house, but how? Jobs were few in his area and how was he to find a job that would bring in the kind of money he had been used to?

John applied for many sales jobs over the next few months. He bought all the national papers looking through the situations vacant section; he registered with all the employment agencies and contacted many companies direct. Many of these applications were successful and he attended many interviews, many of which offered him a job. NONE of which could offer him the kind of money he would need to keep his family and pay the bills.

After four months and many trips to the job centre he and Amy came to the conclusion that they were in deep shit, but what was the best way out?

Thursday and *Daily Telegraph* day, John had great faith in the *Telegraph*. He had always found it a great source of potential jobs in sales at the salary he was looking for. Unfortunately like him, all the true professionals in their field looked in the same paper so competition was fierce, although he considered himself, and was considered to be one of the best in the business.

It was this particular Thursday his eyes came to rest on an advert for a sales manager in Lancashire and Cheshire. The salary was good, commission first class and the opportunity of earning the kind of money he had been used to if not more. The only problem was the area – they would have to live in the area or be prepared to move to even be considered for the position.

It was ten days later when the post dropped through the letterbox and the letter that he was waiting for arrived inviting him for an interview at the Piccadilly Hotel in Manchester.

That night he and Amy went out to the Duck for a drink and to discuss the hopefully pending job. After a few drinks they had both agreed that should he be successful and get the job they would sell the house they were now living in and move up north. Not that they had much choice as by now all their savings had gone and the mortgage was well in arrears.

Two days later John was driving up the M6 on the way to Manchester and to the all important interview.

The interview went well and he considered he had a fair chance of success. Although the company was in the communication industry, which John only had a little knowledge, he considered that his history and considerable proved success in sales could sway them to offer him the position. Well he would know within the week.

John had been out all day meeting people he knew just in case he was not successful in his interview in Manchester. He arrived home about 3.30 to find Amy in the kitchen preparing their evening meal, and as usual a drink waiting for him as Amy had always done.

Amy looked at John and said, "Drink over there on the worktop."

"Cheers," he said as he went across to the large scotch waiting for him. It was then he noticed a letter that bore the logo of the communication company he had the interview with. He picked up his glass and the unopened letter.

"Well open it," Amy said. John took a large drink from his glass and with his heart thumping began to open the envelope, unfolding the paper inside he began to read the contents:

'Dear Mr Davidson

May we take the opportunity of thanking you for attending the interview for the position of sales manager with our company and should like to offer you the position, terms as discussed at the interview.

If I could ask you to contact me on the receipt of this letter, to allow us both to agree a start date and make arrangements for your induction training.

May I wish you every success in your future with our company.

Yours sincerely'

John stood there and read it again.

"Well?" Amy said. "Tell me. I have been waiting all day."

"GOT IT, got the bloody thing."

Amy ran over to him and threw her arms around his neck, "Well done darling, I knew you would."

First thing the following morning he was on the phone to his new company and talking to the sales director. He was on the phone for about half an hour as Amy sat by his side trying to make out what the conversation was about. He put the phone down and with a big smile on his face turned to Amy and said, "Well that's it, start week after next, they are sending confirmation of salary etc. by post today. The only thing is I will be away for three weeks as they want me in the area for training."

Amy looked a little glum but said, "That's not so bad, you will be home at weekends."

"Must phone my mother," John said, "to give her the good news."

"Hi Mum, got good news for you," he then started to tell his mother Dorothy all about the new job and how they would be moving up north. After he had concluded telling her, Amy noticed that most of the conversation had been coming from his mother with the occasional 'yes', 'are you sure', 'that sounds good', 'I am sure Amy will think it's a great idea', 'will phone you later', 'bye', and with that he replaced the phone.

"Well what was that all about?" Amy said.

John looked at her with a broad grin on his face. "You are not going to believe this," he said, and started to tell Amy what his mother had just suggested. "My mother has plenty of room in her house. She said why not move in with her until we get ourselves sorted out. And a house is coming up on a six month lease that a friend of hers owns and she is sure, she could get it for us. That would give us time to sell this house and take our time looking for a new one."

"That sounds great," Amy said. "That means we will not have to be apart and you will be on your area." They smiled at each other.

35

John said, "Let's do it. I'll give her a ring back and ask her to get on with things and tell her we will be up in about a week's time."

They had arranged for all the contents of the house to be transported up to Manchester and stored. John's mother had sorted a new school out for Emma, and here they were an hour from John's mother's and the start of a new life once again.

They settled down quickly at Dorothy's and were looking forward to the holiday in Greece, which was only three weeks away, and on their return moving into the new house they had rented.

John finished his induction training in his new job and completed his first week working on his own; by then it was time to set off on their journey to Bristol to catch the flight to Greece.

p. 15-16 *p. 37-39*

Chapter 5

Interrogation Scene

John looked at the two police officers with his mind racing. What on earth were two members of the West Midland police force doing one hundred miles from their office to ask him about a house?

— "Yes," John replied. "I did buy a house on Crown Road some time ago but never moved into it."

— "Why we want to speak to you is about the house you also purchased on Lynn Road. You DID buy a house on Lynn Road?"

— "Yes," said John.

— D.C. Simons handed him a piece of paper and said, "Could you please look at the signature on the bottom of that mortgage application form." John's head exploded. NOW he had a good idea what this was all about, he looked down at the bottom of the form as D.C. Simons asked him, "Is that your signature?"

— "Yes," John replied.

— "Thank you," the officer said. "Now will you please look at the fourth line from the top? As John's eyes went to the line his stomach churned, the line read, IS THIS YOUR FIRST APPLICATION FOR A LOAN FOR THE PURCHASE OF A PROPERTY, YES/NO. "Do you understand what that question means?" the officer said.

— "Yes," John replied, now with a bit of panic setting in.

— "And what have you put down against that question, John?"

— "That this is my first application for a loan," he replied feeling a little bit better now as the policeman had called him by his first name.

— "That is not correct though, is it?"

— "Well no, but I never moved into the house on Crown Road so I didn't think it mattered."

— "So you admit that you knowingly obtained a loan for a property known as number 10 Lynn Road, Bourneville knowing that the loan was obtained on false information given by yourself?"

— "Well yes," John replied, "but I didn't think it was such a big deal, as Crown Road was taken back by the building society, and the repayments have been paid on Lynn Road, so no harm has been done."

— D.C. Simons turned to D.S. Gill and nodded his head. "John Davidson, I'm arresting you for obtaining money by fraud, contrary to the 1971 theft act. You are not obliged to say anything but anything you do say…"

— John did not hear the rest of the caution his brain went numb. "But I did not know it was all that illegal, after all as I understand hundreds of people do this."

— Neither of the police officers replied apart from saying, "Do you understand the charge?"

— "Yes," John replied. "What happens now?"

— "Well John, you will be released on police bail pending a court hearing at a future date that you will be informed of."

— John's heart was pounding and did not want to ask the next question but knew he had to. "What will happen? I mean what will I get? Is it a fine or is it a custodial offence?"

— "It's not for us to say, but in normal circumstances it is a custodial offence. I recommend that you consult a solicitor as soon as possible."

— After going through all the degrading procedures of having his fingerprints taken, photos taken and signing a form to say that he understood the bail terms, he walked down the steps of the police station having said goodbye to the police officers and to John's surprise one of the officers shook his hand, wished him luck and thanked him for being so cooperative thus saving them a lot of time.

John sat in the car looking at the charge sheet still unable to comprehend what had gone on during the past two hours. What the fuck am I going to tell Amy and my mother he thought? He knew that they would be at home waiting for him, but he needed a bit of time to get his head together.

After a few drinks at the pub he decided he could not put it off any longer and had to break the news to them.

As he walked in the lounge of his mother's house, Amy and his mother looked at him with questions on their faces.

"Well?" Amy said. "What was it all about?"

John started to tell them about all that had gone on at the police station with the intent of not mentioning the possible custodial sentence, but when Amy asked him what was going to happen and demanding the truth, he decided he could not keep the awful truth from her.

"Well I could get a jail sentence, but it would be unlikely and a very short one he lied." Amy and his mother said nothing but just stared at him for what seemed to be forever.

Amy said, "What's this about this house on Crown Road?" John started to tell her all about the purchase of the house and how he could not take her and the children to live in the area. When he had finished she looked at him and said, "YOU BLOODY FOOL! Why didn't you tell me before? You know I would have stuck by you and we would have sorted it out the right way."

"Sorry," John said, feeling like a naughty child that had been scolded for stealing sweets.

Later in the day, John was driving down Oldham Road to see Andrew Blake of A Blake and Co. Solicitors, a name he had got at random from Yellow Pages.

"Sit down," the solicitor said. "You told me a little over the telephone. Suppose you start at the beginning and we will take it from there." John told him all about Crown Road and the first loan, and the full story right up to today. "We have got ourselves into a bit of bother haven't we?" which John thought was rather patronising.

"Certainly have," he replied, "but can you help me and act on my behalf if it comes to court?"

"There is no IF about it," the solicitor said. "They will not let this go." With that he got up off his chair and went over to a large bookcase with hundreds of books on the shelves, chose one sat back at his desk. He looked through the book for some time before closing it and looking at John. "I am not going to pull any punches," he said. "This is a serious charge, and before you say it I know, false applications are done every day and they are hard to detect, that is why when they do find someone the courts tend to make an example of them."

John said, "Example what do you mean?" As soon as he said it he realised what a bloody stupid question it was, he was fully aware of what an example meant.

"What I mean," the solicitor said, "is that it is pretty certain they will impose a custodial sentence."

John's heart dropped and he found it hard to ask the next obvious question. "How long?"

"Twelve months to four years," the solicitor said looking him straight in the eyes, "but I feel it would be more towards the lower end of the scale."

"Christ," John said feeling physically sick.

"Do you wish me to act on your behalf Mr Davidson?" Andrew Blake said.

"If you would," John said, "but if you are, can we work on a John and Andrew basis?"

"Sure," the solicitor said, "No problem."

John arrived home where Amy was waiting for him. "How did you get on?" she said with a worried look on her face.

"Not good," he said. "There is a small possibility of a short prison sentence," he lied.

"What happens now?" she said.

"All we can do is wait and see if it goes to court," knowing there was no IF.

They moved into their new house a week after the meeting with Andrew Blake. John continued to do very well in his new job in spite of what was hanging over him, the daily dread of the post each morning, but in a perverse way wanting the summons from the court to arrive and get this fuck up out of the way one way or another.

Four months went by and nothing came, John was feeling carefully optimistic. Maybe they had decided not to prosecute or maybe they had lost all the paperwork, after all, even the courts could fuck up. Next day the post dropped through the letterbox, and there it was, a large brown envelope. He picked it up and began to open it just as Amy came down the stairs.

You are summoned to appear on the 21st of October in Birmingham Crown Court at 10.00 in the forenoon.

"Well, they didn't forget me after all," he said to Amy surprisingly with a smile on his face. He thought this might lessen the impact for her. "Well, next month it will be all over."

The next two weeks were made up of working, trying to block out the pending court case and visits to see Andrew Blake, who although seemed to work hard on his behalf still gave him the feeling that he had about as much chance as a snowball in hell of getting out of this in one piece.

The evening of the 20th of October was soon upon them, as they sat together having a drink. His mother was with them; she was staying overnight to give Amy some moral support the following day. John had been doing a lot of thinking over the past few days and decided on the best way to protect his family if things went wrong.

"If things go wrong tomorrow you are NOT to visit me under any circumstances, I am not having you have to go to a place like that." He still could not use the word PRISON. "Do you understand?" he said. "And as far as the neighbours are concerned, I have unexpectedly had to go to America for a while on company business, (little did he realise the power of the press) this will save any finger pointing in the street. "Oh by the way, the company knows nothing of this so if it goes well, which I am sure it will (lies) I will be back at work without any slur on my name. If it goes tits up they are bound to telephone to find out why I have not reported into the office, in that case you will have to come clean and tell them."

The morning of the 21st arrived and they were all up early ready for John to set off to Birmingham. They were all in a very sombre mood and John was feeling very nervous about the forthcoming events. Amy noticed this and came over to him with two small pills in the palm of her hand. "Take these," she said.

"What are they?" John said as he looked at the two blue pills in her hand.

"Ativan," she replied. "I took them to calm my nerves after our break up."

John was not into taking pills; nevertheless he took them out of her hand. "Thanks," and gave her a kiss. "I will take them later."

John kissed all of them goodbye, held them all very close. "See you later," he said with a great deal of apprehension.

John was half way down the M6 when for some reason a flood of fear came over him. He pulled into a service station to settle himself down and remembered the two pills Amy had given him. Amy, he thought, when will I see her again? He thought with a sense of real understanding of the possibility of a prison sentence, he swallowed the two pills and resumed his journey to meet what fate lay ahead of him.

He arrived at the courthouse at 9.00 a.m. feeling as if he had just drunk a few dozen whiskeys but very calm (later John was to realise the effect of Ativan). He entered the reception, and was greeted by Andrew Blake, who shook his hand and asked him if he was OK.

"Great," John said, in a none convincing way.

"We are in court one," Andrew said. "Come on, we are first on."

Andrew went into court one and John stayed outside feeling even more pissed; he just wanted to get it over and done with. Fifteen minutes later a tall guy in black robes came out of the courtroom, "JOHN DAVIDSON," he said in a very loud voice.

"Yes, that's me," John replied, he gave him instruction where to go and to stand in the dock facing the judge.

He stood in the dock facing a rather stern looking man in red robes and a short white wig. Due to the effects of the Ativan he was a bit oblivious of the next hour. He remembered placing his hand on a bible and swearing to tell the truth. He remembered the charges being read out to him and a question put to him which prompted a "GUILTY" response. He also remembered Andrew speaking.

What he did remember was the judge summing up, looking at him and saying, "I sentence you John Davidson to 18 months in prison of which I am going to suspend for 12 months. TAKE THE PRISONER DOWN."

A police officer suddenly appeared at the side of the dock and opened the door for him to come out. He immediately took hold of John's arm and there was a click as he was handcuffed to the officer. He was marched off down some steps in a state of shocked disbelief; he was still aware and able to work out that 18 months less 12 months left 6 months he was to be locked away from his wife and children.

He was standing in front of a desk with a large man in uniform behind it. The handcuffs had been removed by now. "Empty your pockets," the man behind the desk said. John started to do as he was instructed and placed all the items on the desk in front of him. At one point he felt a little faint and had to hold on to the desk. "Get your bloody hands off the desk," the voice of the man behind the desk.

John's natural response was to say, 'Go fuck yourself', but stark reality was starting to creep in and he kept his mouth shut. He was then escorted to a cell and told to sit down. He did as he was told as the door closed with a bang and a key was turned in the lock.

He sat there not knowing how long, but long enough to think about 6 months in the situation he was now in. Six months behind bars, 6 months away from all he loved most. It was then he decided what he had to do to survive the mental torture. Whenever he felt like screaming at not being with his loved ones he immediately had to put them out of his mind and concentrate on something else, (as time went by this proved to be the only way for him to keep sane).

The door of the cell opened and a uniformed man stood in the doorway. John was soon to recognise this uniform well as a prison officer's uniform. "Out," the man said. He stood up and was once more escorted through the cell into a large yard where there was a large white van and men waiting to board it. All around were a number of prison officers. Soon it was his turn. He was taken up the steps of the van and noticed all along each side were doors. He was taken to one of these doors, which was opened by one of the officers, put inside and the door locked.

- consider adding a narrative voice over to the piece
- Could voice over mention the A team

"So it was all over, but you haven't even heard how it all began."

"That was it. It was finally over, just like that. But you don't even know what it is, so why don't we go from the beginning."

Chapter 6

The journey to Greenwell prison took, as he estimated, about half an hour. As he walked down the steps of the van he looked on the tall grey walls and bars on all of the windows. They were all taken into a large reception area where they were told to strip and put all their clothes through a mesh covered area where an officer put them in brown bags. John was his name; he was then ushered into a large shower area where he was ordered to shower from head to foot. It was then he realised that any form of privacy for the next 6 months was flying with the fucking dickey birds.

After drying himself off he was marched into a room filled with all kinds of things laid out on tables with guys wearing the same clothes as he was about to be given. Shirts with blue stripes, denim jeans, black shoes, blue ties, socks in fact everything to clothe him. After asking his size he was ordered to dress and marched with the others to yet another waiting area and told to sit down on one of the green metal chairs. One by one they were ushered into another room. John entered to be confronted by a man in a white coat and a prison officer. He was soon to realise that the one in the white coat was the prison doctor. "Sit down," he said to John, again he did as he was told. He had in a short time realised he would have to do as he was told for some time to come.

The doctor started to ask him various questions. "Do you take drugs?"

"No," he replied.

"Are you on any medication?" and so forth. He took his temperature, pulse, weighed him, and then told him to bend over and drop his trousers, after inserting two rubber clad fingers up his backside. He wondered if this was for his benefit or the prison doctor's bit of fun (he found out later this was to check for concealed drugs).

The next thing he was outside the perve doctor's chamber of horrors and being marched along a corridor with metal doors with small peep holes in them. "Stop, Davidson," the escort said, and opened the door in front of him. "INSIDE." With a little push John was inside the cell and looking at a small unshaven man of about 30 years of age.

"OK?" the man said to John.

"Not bad under the circumstances," he said.

"Wot yer infor?" the man said.

"Fraud," he replied.

"Wot yer get?" the man asked.

John assumed he meant what sentence he had received, "18 months 12 months suspended."

"Fucking part-timer eh," the man said with not an unpleasant smile on his face, and held out his hand to John, which he took. "Name's George," the man said. "Welcome to your new home."

"Thanks a lot," he said to the man. "My name's John."

"You're on the top."

John looked around the cell and fixed his eyes on a single double bunk bed. "No problem," he replied.

"Been in before?" his cell mate asked.

"No," John replied.

"Piece of piss for you mate," George said. "You will be sent to the holiday camp before long."

John looked at him and said, "Holiday camp? What holiday camp?"

"Sunlee open nick in Cheshire. I got no chance third time in nick, stuck in this fuckin rat trap for the next 2 years or maybe a bit less if I don't piss on the boots of one of the screws, four months of playtime for you my old son."

"SIX," John corrected him.

"Oh you intend to fuck up then?"

"What the hell are you talking about?" John said.

"Fuck me, you really don't know do yeh?" the man said. "One third off if you are a good boy, tell you fuck all when you first come in, save that for the governor's party time chat with you tomorrow."

"Chat?" John said.

"Yeh, always has a chat with all his new guests to tell them all the rules and how all his little soldiers will look after you and tuck you up in bed at night."

About half an hour later the door of the cell opened and a screw (he was picking up prison jargon quite well in such a short time) stood in the doorway. "Grub," he said and with that went to the next cell and repeated himself.

"Come on," John's cell mate said. "Let's see what shit they have for us tonight." They walked down the corridor and into a very large room with other men dressed like himself stood in a row, which they both joined waiting to be served by about six men behind large pans and trays. He picked up one of the metal trays that were piled up at the end of the serving tables. Each tray had four separate sections in it and proceeded to follow the line of men until a spoonful of mashed potato landed on his tray followed by something which resembled stew and then cabbage.

John then noticed there was nowhere to sit and eat. He turned to George, and said, "Where do we eat?"

"Back at home," he said and with that started back to their cell. John followed, just as they approached the door of the canteen George turned to John and said, "If you want salt it's in the box on the floor by that screw's feet."

"The FLOOR?" John said. "Why the fucking floor?"

"Just another way of making you bow down to the bastards," George said.

He decided he could manage without salt.

They sat on their bunks and ate in silence apart from the few odd words from George which contained words like "crap" and "shit."

"Good day tomorrow," the voice came from below him as he lay on his bunk.

Good day? How can this place have a good day, he thought. "What do you mean good day?" he asked the man on the bottom bunk.

"Pay day, pay day."

"What do you mean pay day?"

"We get four pounds tomorrow so we can give it back to them in the prison shop."

"I didn't know we got a PAY DAY," John said.

"How the hell do you think we get our backy and sweeties?" he said. "Normally you have a job in nick and you get paid but 'cos we 'aven't got a job they give us money for nothing, like getting the dole, good int it, and you can go walkies as well."

"WALKIES?"

"Yeh ours is eleven till twelve. We walk round and round for a fucking hour and then bang, back home until the next day. Night, see you at six."

John slept badly, his mind kept going to Amy and the children, each time trying to put his thoughts out of his head, but no matter how he tried his mind continued to drift back to his loved ones.

Six o'clock came and the door of the cell opened, George got off his bunk and started to dress. "Come on," he said to John, "brecky time."

John followed him in getting dressed and noticed George had collected his toothbrush and paste out of the small cupboard on the wall. John followed him and collected his. They walked out of the cell onto the corridor and John followed him across the landing and through a door opposite the cell. It was a large room with rows of washbasins where a dozen or so men were washing and cleaning their teeth. At the far end of the room there were rows of toilets some of which had men sat on the seats.

John turned to George and said, "Why don't they close the doors?"

"Doors? What doors?" John looked at him after noticing there were no doors on the cubicles. George smiled at him, and said, "See mate, just another way the bastards try to turn you into a fucking animal."

John went to the next vacant washbasin and washed and cleaned his teeth, then proceeded to one of the toilet cubicles. Now he did feel that all kind of privacy and dignity had been stripped away from him. They finished in the washroom and went down the corridor back to the canteen they had been in the previous night. Breakfast was not bad and John had bacon and eggs with a round of toast and a cup of cold tea, again eating it on his bunk. It was about an hour later, the door opened again and George said, "Come on, time to go shopping," and with that started for the door. John followed him on to the landing and down the corridor into yet another room; at the end was a mesh cage with one of the screws behind. George went to the cage with John following him, "3302," George said.

"Four pounds," the screw said as he looked in a large red book.

"12 grams of puff, matches, an extra letter and a pack of papers," George said.

"22 pence left on the book," the screw said. "Leaving it on or spending it?"

"Leave it on," George said.

John went to the cage when George had collected his things.

"Number?" the screw said to John.

"I don't have one," he replied.

"Name?"

"John Davidson."

The screw looked up at John with a sarcastic smile on his face. "Thank you JOHN, but just Davidson will do." With that went to another book and looked down the pages. "What do you want? MR Davidson," he said again with a sarcastic smile on his face.

John took George's lead and asked for the same, "22 pence left on the book."

"Leaving it or spending it?"

He again took George's lead, "Leave it on."

Back in the cell John said, "What was that all about?"

George replied, "Shopping day." John looked down on his bed at the things he had purchased: a sheet of paper and an envelope both stamped with the words HER MAJASTY' PRISON GREENWELL. "What have I got this for?" he asked.

George looked up at him deciding it was time to help him out after all he was a novice in the nick and he had many years of knowledge behind him. "Right, ye get two blank sheets of writing paper a week to write to your nearest and dearest. If you want to write more letters you can buy 'em like you and I 'av just done, the puff is to roll up, stick in yer mouth and set fire to wiv the matches you 'av got."

"I don't fucking smoke," John said.

"START it will give you somethin' to do for the next few months."

It was about two hours later when the cell door opened, "Davidson," the screw in the doorway said. "Governor's meeting," and gestured John to come out of the cell. John went outside and followed the man down the corridor to the reception area and outside a large door with a sign saying GOVERNOR.

The screw knocked and opened the door, took John's arm and escorted him inside. At the back of the room sat behind a large desk was a rather imposing man with grey hair. "Davidson," he asked.

"Yes sir," John replied, thinking to add the sir for some reason, although he never believed in calling anyone sir unless they had received a knighthood. He stood in front of the desk with his escort at his side.

"Davidson. I am the governor of this prison and the purpose of this meeting is to tell you what your rights are and what is expected of you. You have received an 18 month sentence of which 12 months have been suspended. That means you will serve a custodial sentence of 6 months which will be reduced to

4 months if you behave yourself, the exact period is 16 weeks and 4 days, do you understand?"

"Yes sir," John replied.

"Taking in the fact that this is your first offence and the nature of the offence, within a short while you will be transferred to an open prison for the duration of your imprisonment. The rules are different to here and they will be explained to you by the governor of that prison when you get there. While you are here, stick to the rules and obey all orders given to you by the officers. Failure to do so will result in transfer to an open prison being withdrawn, do you understand?"

Once more John said, "Yes sir."

"Now you will go with this officer to complete some forms and receive further instructions, dismissed."

John followed the officer out of the governor's office and into another small office with a desk and two metal chairs. "Sit down," the man said. As he did so, the screw sat down opposite him. He handed John a sheet of paper and said to him, "That form I have just given you is to disclose any debts that you have outstanding and any court appearances you have outstanding."

John looked down at the sheet of paper and took the pen from the man in front of him. He could understand the pending court appearances but could not understand the debt. "May I ask a question?" John said.

"Yes what is it?" he asked.

"Why do you wish to know what debts I have?" John was amazed at the explanation.

"Well," the man said, "as you have received a custodial sentence you cannot leave prison with any debts which may encourage you to commit another crime on your release to pay off those debts, therefore all debts will be settled on or before your release."

Fuck me, John thought, that's a bonus thinking of the few bob he owed the bank and a few H.P. agreements he had. After about ten minuets the form was complete and he handed it back to the officer who looked over it. The man looked at it and then turned to John with a smile on his face. "Not bad," he said. "Got more than that myself, want to put some of mine down?" he said with an even bigger smile.

Not bad this screw, John thought, even seems to be human.

"Next thing we have to do is to let you know the rules of your stay with us." He then began to tell him about exercise time, smoking, etc. He then went on to say, "Your new name is 3708 that you must remember, if you are asked your name from now on it is not John Davidson, but 3708 Davidson, do you understand?"

"Yes," he replied, and with that was led back to his cell.

Time went slowly for John over the next week, giving him more time to think of Amy and the kids, which screwed his head up, wondering how they were and what they were doing. The only highlights were the walks around the exercise yard, round and round and fucking round, but at least out of that bloody cell. Sunday was good, it meant that he could get out for an extra hour attending the church service in the large hall; otherwise it was 23 hour lock up, reading books that came round once a week on a trolley, most of which were cowboy books. He hated cowboy books but he read every fucking one. When he had nothing to read, just for something to do he would guess how many o's were on a page and then count them to see how near his guess was.

Every day he waited for the cell door to open and someone to tell him he was going to be moved to the open prison he had found out was called Sunlee, but day after day nobody came.

Half way through his second week he was making his way back from the canteen when he was stopped by the decent screw who had more debts than he had. "Moving tomorrow," he said.

"Moving?" John said, "where to?"

"Sunlee," he said again with that smile on his face.

John could not believe it; at last he was going to be out of this hell hole.

Seven thirty in the morning John was in the reception dressed in his own clothes looking at a graffiti covered wall with, including many other were, 'IF YOU CAN'T DO THE TIME, DON'T DO THE CRIME', and 'THE BEER IN THIS PLACE IS LIKE MAKING LOVE BY A RIVER, FUCKING CLOSE TO WATER'. John smiled to himself feeling great to be on his way out of Greenwell. There were 12 other guys in the reception all with a smile on their faces, some of whom he recognised from his arrival. They waited for about an hour until one of the screws came in and said, "Right let's go." He ushered them all into the reception yard where a large coach was waiting for them. A coach, John said to himself, not a prison van but a bloody coach. They all got on one by one and sat down.

John sat next to a tall slim guy with red hair. "Hi," John said to the man. "I'm John."

"Pete," the man replied with a smile. "Nice to be out of that fucking place," he said.

John said, "Been told this Sunlee place is like Butlins."

"Sure is compared to this place," Pete said pointing to the gates of Greenwell.

"Do you know Sunlee?" John said to the man next to him feeling that in his reply he had been there before.

"Yep, two years ago, spent six months in there, toe the line and it's a piece of piss."

Chapter 7

It took about one and a half hours to get over the Cheshire border heading for his new home at Sunlee. John felt quite excited at the prospect, excited, what the fuck are you thinking? You are still in nick and away from your family, what the hell is exciting about that?

They entered the village of Sunlee. John noticed it was a beautiful rural village with a superb Elizabethan manor house set in the centre. How the fuck did they get planning permission to build a nick here, John thought. They turned off the main road and on to a B road which led them to the entrance of Sunlee open prison.

The first thing he noticed were the walls, there were none, at least not to speak of, just a two foot wall going round the perimeter. They turned into the entrance and towards a large gate with a small brick building on the left hand side. The gate opened and the bus stopped to be approached by a uniformed man from the gatehouse. The driver gave him a sheet of paper and was then waved on down the drive of the prison. The bus stopped outside a building with a cross over the large front door which turned out to be the prison chapel. As they got of the bus, they all stood around taking in their new home.

"An aviary," John said to Pete, who had said very little during their journey. "They have a fucking aviary with various coloured birds flying around inside."

"Yep," Pete said. "Last time I was here one of my jobs was to look after them. I hope I can pull that job again," he said.

"Follow me," a voice said from behind them as the screw started towards a large wooden building at the side of the church. They followed him into the building which contained row upon row of clothes, shoes, boxes of toothbrushes, in fact everything they would need for their stay in their new home.

They were ordered to line up by a large table behind which stood five or six prison officers. One by one, they were asked the size of their waist, neck, shoes, and everything else to fit them out with a full uniform. They were given bed sheets, pillows, all the things for their future comforts.

"Well, hello again," one of the screws said to Pete.

"Hello Mr Anderson," Pete replied.

"Nice to see you back," the screw said.

"Sorry I can't agree with you sir," said Pete.

They were then ordered to change from their own clothes and into the ones they had just been given. After a short while they all stood there in their new clothes and their own clothes were put in large brown paper sacks each with their names and number on.

The screw who knew Pete from his last visit, turned to him and said, "Well 3302 you know the score, why not take your new bed mates over to 'A' dorm and I will be over in about half an hour."

"Yes sir," Pete replied.

He turned to John and said, "Come on follow me." John did and all the others followed Pete across the yard past the aviary where they stopped for a short while for Pete to say hello to his old friends, then they proceeded along the road past a building which said DOCTOR and then through a large green door which led them into a long corridor about 100 yards long with windows running down the left hand side over looking well kept gardens. About 20 feet up the corridor, they turned went through a large doorway and into 'A' dorm. It was about 30 feet long with large metal cross sections supporting the roof. Down both sides of the room were beds with wooden lockers at the side. Windows ran the full length of the building, and NO bars. On the left hand side, there was a washroom with showers and a line of toilet cubicles WITH doors. At the side of that was a small room containing a large water boiler. There was also a large fire door at the bottom of the dorm.

"Choose a bed," Pete said. "But not on the left hand side, the best ones are at the far end." With that, Pete walked to the last bed on the right hand side and threw his bedding on the metal bed. John followed him and took the bed next to him.

"What happens now?" John said to Pete.

"Well the first thing is to make up our beds." He started to make up his; after about 15 minutes every one had followed Pete's lead and were standing around talking.

"Good day," once more the voice of the screw said, as he walked in. "I see your brother in arms has shown you the ropes of getting settled in. I am now going to instruct you what is going to happen during the next few days, but don't get settled in here too well, this dorm is just for our new guests until you are assessed. Today you can find your way round, tomorrow you will see the governor for his pet talk. You will also have a meeting with the officers and civil people who will assess what jobs you are most suited to undertake. On the wall at the bottom of the dorm," he turned and pointed to a large piece of cork fastened to the wall with various sheets of paper pinned on, "is a notice board, that will tell you all the do's and don'ts while you are in here. I suggest you read them and if you have any questions, address them to an officer or to your blue band whose room is over there," and pointed to a door at the entrance to the dorm, "and with that I will let you settle in." He turned and walked out of the dorm.

"What's a blue band?" John said to Pete.

"A blue band my son, is a trustee, who is responsible for the running of the dorm, normally someone who is serving the last stretch of a murder rap."

"MURDER?" John said.

"Yep that's right." John was taken back for a few minutes at the thought of a convicted murderer was responsible for the running of the dorm.

John walked over to the notice board and started reading the various sheets of paper fixed to it, meal times, work start times, time for parade each morning, but what caught his eye more than anything was a list of all the people who had arrived today and the anticipated date of release. He went down the list until he stopped at Davidson 3708 A.D.O.R. (anticipated date of release) 27-02-1982. This brought him down to reality once more, and once more his thoughts went to Amy and the children. These were interrupted by Pete standing behind him saying, "Come on, let's give you a guided tour."

Pete walked out of the dorm with John on his heels. They turned right and started to walk up the long corridor passing other dorms with letters over the entrances 'B', 'C', 'D', and so on until they finished at 'K'. They eventually got to the top of the corridor which branched off to the right and left.

"Come on," Pete said. "I will show you the games room first," With that turned and walked down the left side. Pete got to a door and walked in.

"FUCK ME!" John said as he followed Pete inside, "fucking snooker tables, four of them."

"Yep, not bad are they?" Pete said. John went over to the only table that did not have anyone playing on it.

"These are top class," he said to Pete, (he knew his snooker, he had played for many years).

Montage of all the areas

"Only the best my cocker," Pete replied. "Come on, let's show you the TV lounge," and with that retraced their steps to follow the right hand corridor into another very large room with rows of chairs and at the far end, to John's amazement, was a bloody great TV screen.

"Bloody hell!" John exclaimed. "This is fantastic."

"Yep, the other room is the film room. We get films every week, so if you don't want to watch TV you can see a film, restricted of course," he said. "For instance you will never get *The Great Escape*," he said with a smile.

They walked out of the doors at the other end of the corridor and across the superb gardens to a very large building with large windows that started half way up the walls and finished at the roof.

"Saved the best for last," Pete said again, with a smile on his face. John knew he was enjoying himself showing off his knowledge of the place. As they walked into the building there was a door facing them and a door to the right. They went through the door facing, and in front of them was the best gymnasium John had ever seen. What it did not have you did not need. There were about ten men working-out; some of them obviously spent all their free time in the gym.

"Come on, let's move on," Pete said, and walked back through the door they had just entered. They entered the next door and there before him made John's jaw drop. Again all he could do was once more say, "FUCK ME!" There was a huge sports hall with a highly polished wooden floor marked out in various colours for five-a-side football, badminton, basketball and any other sport you could think of.

"This is fantastic," John said. "Who said it was like Butlins? It's ten times better, all we need is a fucking swimming pool."

"Oh, haven't I told you about the lake just across from 'A' dorm," Pete said.

"You are joking?" said John.

"NO. Show you that later." They were just about to leave when a man in a red and black tracksuit walked over to them. "Haven't seen you before," he said to John, then looked at Pete and said, "but I know you, been naughty again?" he asked smiling and shaking his head. "My name's David Mackinskey I run the sports area of the nick," he said. "I am, as you may say a screw, but don't have anything to do with lock up and things like that. My job is to look after the people who use the gym and help in what way I can." John was surprised he used the word screw and not officer. "Any activity you are interested in?" he asked John.

"Well, John," replied, "I notice that there are some guys playing badminton over there. It's a game I have always wanted to play but don't know the first thing about."

"No problem," the guy said. "As soon as you have sorted yourself out come and see me," and with that turned to walk away, he stopped and turned round to John and said, "by the way, in my section but my section only, people call me Mack," and with a smile walked off.

They sat on their bunks, John said, "What's the catch? There has got to be a down side apart from the fact we are still in nick."

"Yes," Pete said. "Don't go over the wall for a pint."

Twelve thirty arrived. "Come on," Pete said to John, "let's eat." John followed him out of the building and down a narrow road to a path leading to another building with large double doors. There were about twenty guys queuing to get through, and after a couple of minutes they were walking through the doors into a large room lined with tables and chairs, about half of them were taken up with men eating. To the left as they walked in was a long serving area made of stainless steel and lights over it shining on trays of food which at first glance looked pretty good. They collected their trays with the various compartments in and went to be served. The guy dressed in white asked, "Beef, chicken or curry?"

A choice, John thought. After deciding to go for the chicken, he moved on to the next man, "Mash or chips?" he asked.

"Chips please," John said, and moved on to the next man, "Peas or carrots?"

"Peas," John said. He then proceeded further down the serving area where there were slices of bread piled up and a huge metal bowl full of butter with a knife stuck in it. John took two slices of bread and helped himself to a knife full of butter. He looked round to see where he and Pete could sit and chose a table by the window.

"I can't believe this," he said to Pete. "A choice of food and somewhere to sit and eat it." John thought for a moment how quickly his standards had changed. He was in nick, away from his family, sat in a room full of cons, eating out of steel tray with sections in it, surrounded by screws, and he thought it was great. What would he be like after four bloody months?

After they had eaten, which he must admit was bloody good, they both walked slowly back towards the dorm past a building John had not been in before. "What's that?" he said to Pete.

"The library," he told John.

"Is it OK to go in?" he asked.

"Sure go ahead, I'm going back to the dorm to get my head down for a bit," and with that carried on walking.

John stood outside the building not knowing what to do when he went inside or what to expect, after all this was the first time he had been on his own without Pete by his side to give him advice.

He walked through the door to be confronted by a desk and rows of books and various recording devices and computer screens.

"OK mate?" a voice said. He looked at the desk to see a short man in prison uniform with a broad smile on his face, "What can I do you for?" he asked him.

"Don't know really, just arrived and not sure what the script is," John replied.

"Script is, you give me your name and number, you choose what you want, take it away with you and read it, then bring it back in seven days and choose something else."

"What about all this computer and recorder equipment?" John said pointing to a long table with chairs in front of each piece of equipment.

"That's for the clever cunts who want to learn things like Spanish or French and shit like that; we have some things called language courses on computer disc with earphones so you can repeat the shit and play it back, load of bollocks I think, let the fuckers learn to speak our language like what I does."

John made no comment on this guy's grasp of the English language but started to walk past the shelves of books hoping that they were not all cowboy books. To his surprise the selection was damn near as varied as his local library at home, not as many but just as varied. He noticed a book he had read many years ago, 'ON THE BEACH' by Nevil Shute. He decided to take that and read it once more. "Take this one," he said to the short guy behind the desk.

"OK," the man said as he looked at the book. "Looks like a load of shit to me," he said. John considered everything was a load of shit to him. "Name and number?" the man said.

"3708 Davidson," John replied.

"OK," the man said. "By the way, got some great cowboy books, if you want one?"

John just looked at him with a frown on his face and said, "Thanks I'll remember that next time."

He arrived back at the dorm to find Pete lying on his bed. "Got to be at the shop in ten minutes," Pete said. "Got to get our arrival goodies."

"What's that?" John asked.

"Well, they give us the first week basic pay to get what we need until we start a job and get paid."

They arrived at the shop which was as in the other hell hole behind wire with a screw behind. "Next," the screw said and Pete stepped forward.

"Small pack of tobacco, pack of papers, jar of coffee," Pete said.

"12p left, keep it or spend it?"

"Keep it," Pete said.

"Number and dorm?" the screw said as he took hold of a large book.

"3546 'A' dorm," he replied.

"OK, next."

John stepped forward and ordered the same items, gave him his number and dorm and left his 12p on the book.

When they got back to the dorm there was a man going from bed to bed putting sheets of paper with envelopes and plastic razors on each of them, and a large sheet of paper with writing on, John noticed on his left arm he wore a blue band.

As John approached him he said, "You must be…?" hesitated looked at a sheet of paper and said, "Ah. Yes, Davidson 3708."

"Yes," he replied.

"What's your first name?"

"John," he again replied.

"Mine's Barry," the blue band said. "As you may gather," pointing to the band on his arm, "I am the trustee on 'A' dorm. I have seen all the other new guys and told them what the score is. I am responsible for the smooth running of the dorm and to make sure it's always clean and tidy and you guys obey the rules although I can't see everything," he said with a smile on his face. "The main rule is IF you do break the rules in any way, DON'T get caught, otherwise it's my arse on the block. You will get your paper and envelope every Friday and a new razor. The letter can be put in the post room at any time and mail is collected after finish of work every day apart from Saturday and Sunday. I have put some forms on your bed. Could you please complete them and put them on the table outside my room, these are for your assessment for work. If you have any questions just give me a shout, I'm always about when I am not playing badminton."

"Badminton? Had a word with Mack a few hours ago and told him I wouldn't mind having a go at that."

"Great game," Barry said, "come over with me sometime and we will have a game," and with that raised his hand and said, "See you later, nice guy."

John thought, MURDERER? No chance.

John sat on his bed and started to complete the forms, asking all about his work outside, qualifications, hobbies etc. When he had finished he put them on the blue band's table. Back at his bed he started to read his book, but after about half an hour found he could not concentrate and decided to go for a walk around parts of the prison he had not been to. He walked past the sports hall and found himself surrounded by large buildings which turned out to be work shops with a great deal of activity inside. He walked past rows of greenhouses with men working in them, and then to the perimeter wall, he looked across the road and at freedom. He walked for some time without noticing the light was starting to go. He had no idea how long he had been walking or what time it was (watches had been taken off them and put into the large brown sacks with their other belongings).

He looked at the large clock on the wall of the dorm when he returned and was surprised to notice it was fifteen minutes past four. All the men in the dorm were either sitting on their beds or standing around talking waiting for six o'clock and time for their evening meal.

Once more Pete and John were standing waiting to get served in the canteen. This time as well as a main meal there was soup to start and fruit suet pudding for afters, all of which were very good. They sat at the same table as at lunchtime; it seemed like all the others had sorted themselves out into a regular seating place that would more or less stay the same for the duration of their stay. All the men were talking as they ate their meals, then as they were about to leave one of the screws stopped someone going through the door. "POCKET," the screw said to the man, a worried look came over the man's face. "Come on," the screw said, "empty your jacket pocket." The man did as he was ordered and produced a round of bread. "You're on a charge, my boy," the screw said and with that took him outside the building.

"What the fuck was that all about?" John said to Pete.

"Can't take any food out of the canteen," Pete replied.

"Why not?"

"Don't know, just one of the rules," said Pete.

"What will happen to him?"

"Depends if he has been put on a charge before, if he hasn't, just a bollocking, if he has he could lose part of his remission."

"Bit harsh for a piece of fucking bread," John said.

"Doesn't matter if it's a loaf of bread or a pea, same thing."

They sat on their beds when the evening meal was over, some went down to watch TV. John managed to read his book until lights out at 9.30; it wasn't really lights out more of a lights dull. There was still sufficient light to see round the dorm and if you made the effort even read, but John was so tired after the day he had and all the fresh air he soon fell asleep. His last thoughts were, one gone only sixteen weeks and three days to go. He was awakened some hours later by a shout and someone jumping out of bed. What the fuck, he thought, looking to the beds on the other side of the dorm?

Pete sat up and looked at John, "Told you not to choose a bed on that side didn't I?"

"Well, it's a welcome present to the new guys from the guys in 'B' dorm across the way."

"PRESENT?" John asked.

"Yep, they all piss in a bucket, open a window over one of the beds and throw it over the lucky guy. Good night."

Chapter 8

The lights came on at six the following morning and John wondered what was going to happen today? Pete got up and made his way to the washroom, his clothes and shoes under his arms. John followed him about five minutes later. He had a quick shower and dressed himself before going back to his bed where Pete was waiting for him to let him know what would happen next. Although he was just about to start when Barry the blue band appeared at the bottom of the dorm. "Right guys, for those of you who don't know the score, parade is in the yard at seven prompt and I mean prompt, you will see the letters 'A' to 'K' you line up facing 'A'. Do not talk until parade is over, you then come back to the dorm and clean round your bed area. I will see you when you come back and let you know a little more."

Everyone left the dorm and went down to the parade ground and formed their respective line awaiting the PO (principle officer) to arrive. He came about ten minutes later and walked up and down the lines of men. Four more screws were making a head count to make sure nobody had gone walk about during the night. After about fifteen minutes, when they were satisfied they had a full complement of cons, they were dismissed to go back to their respective dorms.

When they arrived back, Barry was waiting for them to show them where brushes, mops, mop buckets etc were kept. "Pass them on to the next man when you have finished with them," Barry instructed. John swept around and under his bed and then mopped the floor. Barry came round to each man's bed area and inspected the cleaning, stopping at only one to point to a mark in the corner and asking him to do it again. "I'll get my arse kicked if one of the screws see that," he said to the man.

When Barry was satisfied with the standard of cleaning, he turned to them all, and said, "Right, after breakfast you have all got to go to the office block to see the governor and to the see the job assessment guys. Then for the next two days your time is your own. Make the most of it, you will all be in some kind of job after that. Oh, by the way, I have put a rota on the board for you all to look at; this is for the purpose of cleaning the dorm, washroom and corridor facing the entrance to the dorm, Mondays, Tuesdays and Fridays. You will see it is fair and you all have an equal amount of time in each area, although I would expect next week you will all go to your new dorms where you will stay until your release."

After a breakfast of eggs, bacon and toast washed down with two cups of tea, John made his way over to the office block, a long narrow building near the gatehouse by the gate lodge. As he entered followed by Pete and other men from 'A' dorm they were met by another screw, who Pete recognised from his last visit to the nick. Pete turned to John and said, "Watch out for that one, he is a first class bastard."

They were shown into a waiting room with various doors, two of which had signs on them, one said GOVERNOR and the other ASSESSMENT.

"Sit," the screw said, with a scowl on his face. One by one they were taken into the governor's office. Soon John was instructed to enter the office and walked in with the screw at his side. There was a large desk with a balding man sat on the other side reading papers that were attached to a red file. He said nothing for a while and then looked up at John and asked, "3708 Davidson?"

"Yes," John replied, he received a dig in the ribs from the screw who said, "sir."

"Sorry," John said, as he repeated his answer. "Yes sir."

"You have been sent here to serve out the remainder of your sentence of six months, as you no doubt know that if you behave yourself that will be reduced by one third. This is an open prison and the rules are few, however all rules will be obeyed without question, do you understand?"

"Yes sir," John replied, remembering not to get another dig in the ribs from the screw.

"You can step over the wall at any time, this is known not as escaping but absconding, but whatever you wish to call it, it means you will be back in Greenwell before your feet touch the ground. Any other breach of the rules will be met with you losing some or all of your remission, do you understand?"

"Yes sir," he replied.

"There are many facilities you can take advantage of during your stay here and I would urge you to take advantage of them, that's all, dismissed."

John returned to his chair in the waiting room and about ten minutes later the door marked ASSESSMENT opened and a voice said, "Davidson." He got up and walked to the open door, this time without the screw following him. As he entered the room he was asked to sit down facing a long desk with two screws and two men in civilian dress. The two men in civvies smiled as he sat down, one of the men then looked back down at the paper on the desk in front of him. While he did so, one of the screws said to him, "The reason you are here is to find the best way you can benefit the prison and yourself while you are serving your term of imprisonment. These two gentlemen are from education and arts departments and are on the board of our education and employment section." The screw looked at the man who was reading the document in front of him which John had noticed by now were the forms he had filled in yesterday and put on Barry's table.

The man looked up at John and smiled, "Quite impressive," he said. "You are a very well educated man, with a great deal of business experience."

"Thank you," John replied not knowing if he should say anything.

"The fact is," the man said, "there are lots of jobs available in here such as joinery work, factory work, laundry and many more and it is our job to make sure we fit you into a position which is the best for us and the best to benefit you. Have you any ideas yourself?" he asked John.

John thought for a while and then said with a smile on his face, "I don't think I would be much good doing any joinery work, I even put screws in with a hammer." John thought using the word screws and hammer could have been phrased a little better; they all gave a slight smile, even the screws.

"Well we all read your file before you came into the room and consider you would fit into our education programme. What do you think?" he said to John.

"Well, er, yes, what does it entail?"

"It's a programme that means you can learn more about the business world, and computers, and take an exam at the end which will give you the B.E.C certificate in business studies. That's what we do for you, what you do for us is help in conjunction with our civilian tutors in the prison, with other prisoners, who to say the least aren't as educated as yourself, to put it bluntly can't even read or write."

John thought this sounds a cushy number in out of the cold, as he glanced over the man's shoulder out of the window to see the first wisps of snow coming down. He turned his attention to the men behind the desk, and said, "Well, yes I think I would get a great deal of satisfaction out of that."

"Good," the man said. "Although I must tell you as you will find out anyway, it's the worst paid job in here – four pounds a week where the laundry and factory work carries six to eight pounds a week."

"That's OK," John replied. "May I ask where is the education department?"

"The door opposite the room you are in now," the man replied, "report tomorrow at 9.00am prompt, any questions?"

"No sir," said John.

"You may go now," the man said. "Best of luck."

John arrived back at the dorm to find most of the guys were standing around discussing what jobs they have been given. Pete came over to him, "Well what did you get?" he asked.

"Education," he replied.

"You jammy fucker," he said. "The best number in the nick."

"And you?" John asked him.

"Grounds maintenance and garden," he replied. "Great in summer but a bastard in winter."

"Right guys," a voice said from behind them. John turned around to see Barry standing in the doorway. "Seems a bit quick, but they have done the dorm allocation. I can only put it down to the fact that it's a day off work today because all the screws are in some kind of meeting. Will put it on the board for you to see where you are going to live, as from now," and with that walked over to the board and pinned a piece of paper to it.

John turned to Barry and asked, "You mean now as now?"

"Yep, collect all your things and report to the blue band on your respective dorms." John walked to the board and looked down the list until he came to his name 'C' dorm it had at the side of his name. Pete was at his side looking down the sheet, "F," he said.

"Well let's go to our new homes," John said, and set off up the dorm to collect his things.

He walked down the corridor and through the entrance to 'C' dorm just as a guy with a blue band on his arm came out of a room. "John Davidson?" the man asked.

"Yes," John replied.

"Welcome to our happy band. Barry told me you would be joining us," he said with a smile on his face. "Bit quick though, normally takes another day or so. Your bed is the third from the top on the right, put your things away and make your bed up and come and see me in my room when you have finished."

John walked up the dorm past all the other beds with some of the men letting on to him and others not even looking up. He put all his things in his locker and made his bed up and returned back down the dorm to the trustee's room by the entrance. He knocked on the door and a voice said, "Come in." John entered the blue band's room to see him sitting on a chair with another in the corner; it was a small room with a table, a bed and some cupboards on the wall. "Grab that chair," the guy said to John. "But before you do, go and put some hot water in those two cups will you?" pointing to two cups on the table containing teabags. John took the cups and went to the boiler room across from the blue band's room. He returned with both cups full of boiling water. "Cheers, milk?"

"Please," John replied as he sat down.

"Right, just tell you a bit about 'C' dorm, exactly the same as 'A'," he said. "But just to let you know about me, I prefer to tell you myself rather than guessing and getting it wrong. I am Phil, and I have been here for twelve months after coming from Strangeways in Manchester where I served five years for murder. I have another two years to serve here. The circumstances of my sentence I will tell you as I have all the others, this way we don't have horrific stories going round of a mass killer in our little group. Briefly I was in a pub in Manchester with my new girlfriend when her ex walked in and came over and gave her slap in the mouth, so I punched him in the face. He then pulled out a knife and came for me. To cut the story short, the knife ended up in my hand and then ended up stuck in his chest, and that is it."

John just looked at him not knowing what to say, but just found him saying, "What a bastard."

Phil looked at him with a smile and said, "Sorry it wasn't more exiting, all the guys in here are spot on, apart from one, and that is Terry in the first bed on the left. He likes to think he is a hard man and likes everyone to know it; try and keep out of his way as much as you can, he is a troublemaker".

The next half hour was spent talking and drinking their tea with some biscuits which Phil had retrieved from a drawer in his cupboard. "Well, got to kick you out now," he said to John. "Got things to do."

John left the room and walked up the dorm towards his bed noticing the dorm was the same as the one he had just left apart from a large table with chairs around it in the centre where a few men were sitting reading and writing letters, a few of them nodded as he went past. He got to his bed to see a small guy sitting on the bed next to his. "Hi, name's Andy," the man said.

"Hi, mine's John," he replied, sitting down on his bed.

"How long you got?" he asked.

"Six months," John said.

"What for?" the man asked again.

"Fraud," John replied, a little taken aback by the questions. Nobody until now had asked about or talked about their convictions or sentence.

"Twelve months me," the man said. "Screwed a garage for some cigs, should 'av bin more clever third time the fuckers 'av 'ad me for screwing garages, 'av to change my target next time."

"If I were you," John replied, "I would do something you are good at."

The man laughed. "A bank maybe," he said, with a broad grin. John thought he was going to like this guy, there was something about his unashamed honesty.

John got his paper and envelope out of his locker and went to the table in the centre of the dorm. He sat down and started to write a letter to Amy telling her all about what had happened and how much he was missing her and the children. When he finished it he put it in the envelope and for some reason decorated the envelope with flowers and vines around the edge, he had always been a very good artist, (little did he know that this skill was going to make his life inside a little more comfortable). When he had finished he looked across the table to a guy who had also been writing, but noticed this man was writing with a superb gold fountain pen. He was looking at the pen when the man looked up and said, "OK?" to him.

"Not bad," John replied.

"Have you got your job yet?" he said to John.

"Yes," he replied. "Starting in the education department tomorrow."

"Education? Same as me," the man said. "Been there for four weeks, it's a good number, pay lousy but a bloody cushy position."

John noticed he spoke very well and appeared to be well educated. "My name's John," he said to the man.

"Garry," the man said, as he leaned over the table and shook John's hand.

"See you later," John said, as he left the table and went back to his bed area.

He lay on his bed trying to put Amy and the children out of his mind without a great deal of success, when a voice from the bottom of the bed said, "Wot you in for?"

Without looking up replied, "Getting caught." He didn't know why he said that it just came out.

"Oh a clever cunt," said the man standing by his bed.

John looked up and said, "If I was I wouldn't be in here." The man did not smile but just walked away.

"Fuck me, he didn't like that." It was Andy who sat on his bed next to John.

"Who is he?" John asked.

"That's Terry," Andy replied. Bloody hell, John thought, that's a good start.

Lunch came and went, he had met up with Pete in the canteen and told him all about his move into 'C' dorm and how he had made a good start with Terry. "Good on you," Pete said. "You will soon learn that you have to stand up to guys like that in here, but don't push him he obviously doesn't give a fuck about losing time but you do. Fancy a game of snooker after chow?" Pete said to John.

"Yes why not?" he said.

They left the canteen and walked down the corridor together towards the games room just as Terry was coming out of 'C' dorm, he looked at John with a sarcastic smile on his face. "Got a girlfriend?" he said as he looked at Pete and John.

"Yeah," Pete said, as he winked at John. Terry just looked at them both looking surprised at Pete's answer. They both continued to the games room ignoring the mutter coming from the troublemaker. "Nasty bastard that," John said to Pete.

"Yeah but pay back always comes in here," he said.

They had four games of snooker of which John won three, all games were very close in spite of Pete saying he was a lousy player. As they were walking out of the room they met Garry coming in. John introduced Pete to him and told him that that Garry was on the education section with him.

"Oh," Garry said to John, "that reminds me, I have put some course paperwork on your bed, thought it would give you a chance to read it before you start tomorrow, and see what we have done over the past four weeks."

"Great," said John. "I appreciate that, I'll look at it when I get back," and with that thanked Garry again and said have a good game.

When John got back to his bed in the dorm he noticed a pile of papers and some books on his bed. He collected them and took them over to the large table to read through them. There were sheets of computer print outs and books on computer programming. Jesus, he thought as he read through them, this is a bit out of my league, he had never had much to do with the more technical side of computers let alone programming. He picked up another book which was the full prospectus of the B.E.C. course which made him feel a lot happier – all about interview techniques, sales, management, conducting seminars and many more all of what was right up his street, but fucking computer programming? As he continued to read through the books and papers, Garry came over to him and sat down at his side. "Everything OK?" he said to John.

"Yes fine, apart from this," as he handed the programming sheets to him. "I am fucked with this part of the course."

"No problem," Garry said. "I am clueless on all the other stuff but good at the computer work, so we work together. You help me with all this, pointing down the index page of subjects and I help you on the computer side, OK?"

"That sounds good to me," John said feeling relieved.

The rest of the day was spent talking to Garry about the education section and Garry giving John a little more insight into the world of computer programming most of which flew straight over his head.

After the evening meal he decided to go to the TV room and watch a documentary on seahorses. I didn't know that the male gave birth to the babies and looked after them, fucking good job I'm not one, he thought.

It was while the adverts were on that he noticed a familiar smell from across the aisle at another row of chairs with men sitting on them smoking cigarettes as he himself was doing, grass! He thought, how the fuck have they got dope in here? (Little did he know that within a very short space of time he would find out.)

He lay on his back on top of the bed covers smoking a cigarette, and talking to Andy who was doing the same. Lights had just gone out and all there was the dull light from the inspection lights. "Tell me something?" he said to Andy. "How the fuck do we get marijuana in here?" and told him about the guys having a smoke in the TV room.

"Get anything mate," Andy said. "Watch this space," he said with a smile.

Ten thirty arrived and the evening check by one of the screws was underway. He walked up one side of the line of beds and down the other, now and again as he passed a bed saying hello to the man either in bed or lying on the top.

"Good screw that one," Andy said. "Closes his eyes to a lot that goes on."

Eleven o'clock came and Andy swung his legs out of bed. He was still fully dressed, and another inmate came over to him. "Ready?" the man said.

"Yep, let's go for it," Andy said, and with that went to the fire door at the end of the dorm. Andy opened the door and went through, the other guy closed it very quietly behind him and came over to the bed at the side of John and lay down on the top. John also noticed that Terry had got off his bed and was walking towards the entrance of the dorm where it joined the corridor.

It was about ten to fifteen minutes later when there was a tap on the window of the fire exit door. The man at the side of John got off Andy's bed and opened the door to let him back in carrying a large box which he shoved under his bed. The door was closed and the man went back to his own bed as did Terry at the other end of the dorm. "Knackered," said Andy, as he lay on his bed breathing heavily.

"What the fuck is going on?" John said to him.

"Parcel run," he replied. John said nothing; remembering his words 'get anything mate', he was intelligent enough to now know how the dope got in the prison.

Andy soon recovered and pulled the box from under his bed and put it on the top of his locker. Some of the men came over to the locker and Andy started to hand out various items to the ones who had placed an order! The box was by now quite empty and all of the men had disappeared to various dark corners of the dorm. "Whiskey and orange?" Andy said to John, as he handed him a cup.

John could not believe what he had just seen. "I don't believe this," he said to Andy, as he took the cup out of his hand.

"Believe it," he said. "Got some puff, about two hundred grams, booze and a lump of blow."

"Blow?" John said to him.

"Yep, dope, make a few bob on this lot," Andy said with a smile.

"What would happen if you were caught?" John asked.

"Big fucking trouble," he replied. "But I never have as yet. Another drink?" he said to John, handing him a bottle with a label on the side saying, 'orange squash, dilute with water'.

"Why not? Fuck it," he said as he took the bottle from Andy's outstretched hand.

Chapter 9

It was again six in the morning when all the lights went on and the screw walked up the dorm. "Wakey, wakey another nice day to have fun," he said. It was the screw who had done the night check that Andy had said was a good guy. As he came up to John and Andy's beds he looked at Andy and raised his eyebrows, "Have a good night' sleep?" he said with a smile. "Hope you had an early night?"

"Yes sir," Andy replied, with no smile on his face. He knew the screw knew what had gone on but why? Why did he not grass them up?

Same as yesterday, shower, dress, shave, parade, breakfast and cleaning, it was when all that this was done when Garry came over to him and said, "OK, ready to go over to the block?"

"Sure," John said, "let's go."

They walked over to the office block, through the door that John had been through to see the governor, and to the door facing the assessment room. John followed Garry through the door of the education department office to be met by a tall man in a blue suit who was sitting by a computer. As they entered, he got up from the desk and walked over to them holding out his hand to John. "Good morning," he said with a smile. John took his hand and returned his smile and greeting. "I'm Grant," he said. "I'm your tutor, come over here and let's have a chat." Just then the door opened and six more men walked in. "Morning guys," the man said. "Carry on with your work while I have a word with our new member." He turned round to one of the men, and said "Don, your turn for coffee I believe."

"Sure," the man said, looked at John, and asked, "How do you like yours?"

"Thanks," John replied, "black, one sugar." With that the man walked off to a small room at the side of the office.

"Right," Grant said as they both sat down at a table at the front of the room, "I just want to refresh my memory," as he took a file from a draw under the table. He was quiet for a short while as he looked at the contents of the file, now and again nodding and saying, "Good." When he had finished he looked up at John, and said, "Quite impressive. I notice in your CV you haven't mentioned anything about computer skills?"

"No," John said. "That's because I don't have many," he replied. "I know how to turn one on and how to get the information from one," John replied, "and that's it."

"No problem," the tutor replied. "With regard to the computers they may be used outside work hours for the purpose of revision and work connected to the course. They are NOT under any circumstances to be used for your own gain on the net or any unauthorised access to the net services, OK?"

"Yes," John replied.

They both got up from the table as the guy came over with two cups of coffee and put them down on the table in front of them. "Thanks," they both said at the same time. He turned to the men sat at individual desks all with computers on a table by the side of each one, and said, "This is John, what I want you to do John, is to tell the guys here all about yourself. We all work together here and all have varied attributes which we share together." With that he sat back down on a chair by the desk, leaving John standing up facing the men.

"Well," he started, "my name is John Davidson. I am here for the next six months, but if I am a good boy about sixteen weeks, two days, nine hours," and looking at the clock on the wall, "twenty-four minutes." This seemed to break the ice as all the men in front of him smiled. John then told him about his work experience, his qualifications (all of which were in sales, marketing and management). He then said, "I would like to tell you about my skills in computer programming. I can sum that up in two words, 'fucking none'." Again this received a smile from the guys in front of him.

"Thanks John," the tutor said, and looked at the men in front of him. "Perhaps you would like to tell John your names and what your particular skills are, that way we all know who to turn to for help and advice on any particular subject we are weak on." Each man in turn stood up and did what Grant had requested. John was amazed at the eloquence of most of them and how educated they were, after they all had their say, Grant said, "OK folks, let's get down to work, today we are going to resume the programming work and I will work with John to try and bring him a little bit up to date to where you are."

Garry sat down with John for the next four hours showing him all the dots, got to, and all the jargon involved in writing computer programmes. At the end of this period it was time for lunch and John had absorbed about two percent of what he had been told. He told himself his brain was not built for this and he was about to look a complete twat.

After lunch they were all back in the office, Garry was at the bottom and said, "Right guys, I have a new project for you which has to be completed within the next three weeks. The object of this project is to start a new business and set up a cycle retail outlet, shall we say in Chester? What I want you to do is to set up a shop from scratch, from bank projections, layout of shop, servicing of bikes, stock systems and everything to make a successful retail business. I have got a folder for you all with all you require, example prices, rental of shop, business rates, money available and things like that. If you would like to come forward and collect the folders you can make a start straight away. I must ask that you work on this as a separate project and not as a joint effort, although I know you will ask for help from each other which I would expect, but at the end of the day I expect a different profile from each of you." They each collected a folder from him and set about their tasks. "You may all take whatever you want from the stationery cupboard as long as you complete the book as to what you have taken."

John set about setting up a cycle shop in Chester, knowing fuck all about bikes but knowing a great deal about business. He worked the rest of the day on the project until it was time to finish and go back to the dorm and await the time to go and have his evening meal.

On his way back to the dorm he joined the queue at the post room and looked on the window to see his name on the sheet of paper to say he had post waiting for him. Great, he thought, a letter from Amy. Sure enough when he reached the end of the queue he was handed a letter with Amy's writing on.

He sat on his bed reading the letter from his wife who said she and the children were missing him like hell, which made him feel so helpless at not being able to do anything about. The letter made Amy feel a little closer to him but also set his mind racing about how long it would be before he would be with her and the children again. He started to feel a little down and tried to pull himself together when Garry came over to him and said, "Want to eat?"

"Good idea," John said, glad at something to take his mind off his loved ones so far away.

Over their meal they discussed the new project, Garry admitting he did not know where to start, John explained to him about starting a new retail business and agreed when they had finished their meal they would get together and set out a business profile which they could both work on in their own rights.

Seven o'clock they were seated around the table in the dorm, after leaving the canteen and John having taken a bump off Terry while they were passing in the corridor although there was plenty of space to pass by. This had been a regular thing over the past few days, but he refused to rise to the bait and ignored it. They worked out a business plan on how to build a retail cycle shop. After an hour John said, "Let's call it a day, fancy a game of snooker until lights out?"

"Good idea," Garry said. "Pissed off with this already," he said, standing up and collecting all his things off the table and taking them back to his locker. John did the same putting all his in a neat pile on top of his locker.

Five to nine and the screw put his head round the door of the games room, "Back to dorm, lights out five minutes," he said. They gave up their game with all the colours still on the table and went back to the dorm. John went past Terry's bed to see him with a smile on his face. As he got to his bed he noticed all the papers that were piled up in a neat pile on his locker were all over the floor. He turned and looked back down the dorm to see Terry still with a smile on his face lying on his bed. John said, "That's it," and turned to walk back down the dorm, an arm came from behind him, it was Andy.

"Leave it," he said. "Too many screws about." John pulled his arm away but took notice of what Andy had said and collected the papers from the floor and put them back in a neat pile on top of his locker again. He looked back down the dorm to see Terry still smiling, one day he thought. He had never considered himself a hard man but having been brought up in a tough area in Manchester without a father to run to, made him very handy in sorting his own problems out.

Morning arrived, and after the morning's ritual of washing and having breakfast, he was once more in the education office. Grant came in followed by a new face. "This is Mr McKay," Grant said. "Mr McKay is the principal over in the education department," he said, "that means he is my boss."

"Good morning," the man said. They all responded with the same 'Good morning'.

"I thought I would make myself known to you, and let you know what is expected from you." John saw something in this man's face he did not like. He could not put his finger on it but there was something. "I expect you all to do your best in this department and not to step over the line, I mean not even a toe I hope you understand that. I know due to the fact you are in here means that you are all accustomed to crossing that line, but I unlike many people feel that you are in prison for punishment not for a holiday; the education department is, in my opinion part of that holiday, which I can, and will cancel at the least breach of the rules." He then turned his back and walked back through the door and closed it behind him, they all looked at Grant eyebrows raised.

"What the fuck was that all about?" one of the guys asked.

"Just to let you know how he felt about you all, and to let you know what a cunt he can be," Grant replied with a smile on his face.

They all went to their respective desks and put their folders on the top. Grant stood at the bottom of the room and said, "Due to the fact you have all been given a task to be completed within three weeks, I have decided it will take the place of the computer programming each morning. I am sure some of you will feel close to tears on hearing this, I am sure you are John," as he looked across at him with a smile.

John took his handkerchief out of his pocket and wiped his eyes. "Sure is boss," John replied.

The day went well and they all got down to the project at hand, breaking for lunch, before he knew it is was time to finish for the day and walked out of the lecture room with Garry along the pathway back to the dorm. "Just going to the post room," John said to Garry, "catch you up later."

John went to the window of the room to check the list to see if any post was waiting for him. As he was looking at the sheet of paper he was aware of someone behind him. He turned around to see Terry. Turning back to the window he noticed that no letter had arrived for him and started to walk back to the dorm. "Not got a letter today?" he heard Terry say. John ignored him. "Must be difficult though writing when you are on your back with your boyfriend on top of you." John remembered very little. All he could remember was the sound of a crunch as his head met Terry's nose, he did not even feel the tooth sinking into his knuckle. He did remember hands pulling him away from Terry and a voice saying, "Fuck off back to your dorm, before a screw comes."

John walked away looking back to see Terry lying on the ground his face covered in blood.

He walked into the dorm to see Garry sitting at the table with all the coursework in front of him. He looked up as John approached him and noticed the blood down the front of his shirt and the blood on John's right hand. "What the fuck?" he said to John, who told him that he just kicked fuck out of Terry. "Get changed rapid and wash up," Garry said. With that, John went to his locker to collect a clean shirt and went to the washroom followed by Garry. "Did any of the screws see what happened?" Garry said to John as they entered the washroom.

"No I don't think so," he replied.

"Thank fuck for that," he said, Garry, helped him clean himself up and said, "better take that out," as he pointed to a tooth in John's knuckle.

When they had finished they went back to John's bed area. "In big trouble now," he said to Garry.

"Maybe not," he replied. "It all depends on what that fucker says."

It was about two hours later that Terry walked into the dorm with a screw at his side. It was the one Pete had warned him about in the office as being a nasty bastard. Terry lay on his bed and John noticed that he had a front tooth missing and what appeared to be stitches in his top lip, and a plaster over his nose. "Line up by your beds," the screw shouted up the dorm. They all stopped what they were doing and lined up by their beds as instructed, the screw addressed them all. "Well men, it appears that he," pointing to Terry, "has had an accident. Just to put you in the picture, he has just come back from the hospital and sustained a broken nose, lost a tooth, a cracked cheek bone and has six stitches in his top lip. He says he fell head first into the post room wall. I DON'T fucking believe him, does anybody have anything to tell me?" he said with a smile. Nobody said anything. "Right my boys, hands out in front of you." He started to walk up the dorm inspecting the hands held out in front of all the men.

John's heart was in his mouth, his brain working overtime thinking of something to say, by this time the screw was in front of him, "Well?" he said as he looked at John's hands, "have YOU had an accident as well?" he said with a sarcastic smile on his face.

"No sir," John replied. "Self inflicted."

"What do you mean self inflicted?" the screw said.

"I felt down at not receiving a letter from my wife and punched a wall," John said.

"I don't believe you," the screw replied. John said nothing, and looked the screw in the eyes. "I intend watching you," he said to him. "I know you are involved in this, but you know, and I know I can't prove it," in obvious frustration turned and walked back down the dorm.

John lay on his bed thinking how lucky he was to have escaped a possible charge. "Fucking great," a voice came from Andy's bed. "Did you really punch fuck out of that bastard?"

"YES," he replied, "now forget it."

After the evening meal, John was lying on his bed thinking about Amy and the children, when Terry arrived at the bottom of his bed. He said nothing but just stood there, all the guys in the dorm had seen this and by now were standing up anticipating something was going to kick off. Phil the blue band had come out of his room and was stood half way up the dorm. John knew he had to win this confrontation. John got off his bed and faced Terry. "Getting dark now," John said to Terry, as he looked through the window of the fire exit door, "let's finish it. I'm going to kick your balls into your fucking mouth," John said as he walked towards the fire door and put his hand on the door to open it.

Terry said nothing, but just looked at John. "Call it a day," he said to John, not wanting to show any signs of weakness.

"Good choice," said John. "Now fuck off." Terry walked away down the dorm to his own bed, followed by jeers from the rest of the dorm. John had made his mark.

John lit himself a cigarette and decided to write a letter to Amy, telling her all that had happened during the past few weeks but leaving out the trouble with Terry. The last thing he wanted was for her to worry, and worry she would if she knew. He finished his letter and decorated the envelope with garlands of flowers just as Garry came to his bed. "Fancy going over to the sports hall and having a go at a game of badminton?" he asked.

John thought for a while and decided against it, pointing to his right hand which by now had swollen to twice the size it should have been. "Think I will pass on that," he replied. "Think I will go and watch a bit of TV until lights out"

"OK," Garry said, "leave it a few days, but I would go to see the medic with that," pointing to John's hand.

"Yeh, first thing after parade tomorrow."

John was waiting outside the doctor's office the following morning having asked Garry to tell Grant the tutor where he was. After a short while the door of the doctor's office opened and John stepped inside to see a tall balding man in a white coat. "Sit down," the doctor said to him. "Name and number?"

"3708 Davidson."

"Ah yes," he said. "One of the officers told me to expect you. Been in a bit of trouble have we?"

"No sir, self inflicted."

"Yes, so I understand," the doctor said, raising his eyebrows as he spoke. "Well better let me have a look." He took hold of John's hand, he moved his fingers one by one and asked if he could bend them. After about ten minutes said, "Well I don't think anything is broken, but I'll strap it up, if you have any further problems or it swells anymore come back to see me."

A short while later John was sitting by his desk in the education department having apologised to Grant for being late. Grant was going through the work they had done over the last few days on the setting up of a retail cycle shop. John as with all the other guys, had done a projected business plan to put forward to a bank, a marketing policy and advertising programme. Grant read each man's ideas out to all the other guys and asked for comments and how each man felt the ideas could be improved upon. John was surprised how all the men had put so much effort and thought into the project. By lunchtime they had one very good business plan made up from various parts of all the men's suggestions.

Lunch came and went, and they were once more sitting at their desks with Grant standing in front of them saying how pleased he was at the standard of work that had been carried out. "Now then," he said, "let's take it a stage further. During the next three days I want you to design a retail floor plan, a workshop area and a manual stock control system. All the material you will require is in the stationery room where you can draw whatever you require to complete the task. I would expect you to work on this during your free time and at weekends to complete it within the three day period. Do any of you have a problem with that?"

"No," they all replied.

"Good, well if you want to get what you require and as you are willing to give up some of your free time, once you have what you want you can all go early to make a start back at your dorms." John was last to go to the stationery room after writing a list of what he required, sheets of A3 card, pens, paper clips etc.

"WOW!" he exclaimed out loud, I feel like a kid in a sweet shop, he thought. In front of him were thousands of sheets of paper, coloured card, boxes of pens, pencils, markers everything to make an artist's dream come true. Grant DID say he could take what he wanted.

Back at the dorm complete with all the goodies from the education department, he sat on his bed deciding where to start. First thing he thought was to put all his booty in his locker, after all he did not want to draw too much attention to himself. As he was doing this, Garry came over to him to ask him for a little help as to where to start. "What the fuck is all that for?" Garry asked.

"For my project," he replied.

"PROJECT? It's a cycle shop we have to plan, not the whole of fucking Woolworth's stores."

"Just thought I would get a bit extra to do some art work on," John replied with a smile on his face.

It was time for evening meal and they had been at the task of planning the shop for about two hours and had completed two shop floor plans one for himself and a different one for Garry so it looked like they had not worked together. They were just about to collect all their paperwork when John looked up to see Terry walking up the dorm towards the table they had been working at. John stood up keeping Terry in the corner of his eye, not wanting to make full eyeball-to-eyeball contact with him. As Terry passed by he threw something on the table in front of John but carried on walking up the dorm saying nothing. John looked down to see a joint on the table. Garry also looked at the roll-up on the desk.

"What the fuck?" John said.

"Just pick it up and acknowledge him," Garry said.

Terry reached the top of the dorm and as he opened the fire door turned and looked sideways at John who looked at him and raised a thumb of thanks.

As they sat eating John said, "What do you make of that?"

"A peace offering without losing anymore face," Garry replied. "He had one of two choices, to have another go and hope he would come out on top, which he obviously doesn't fancy his chances or to make the peace slowly, slowly without too many people seeing. I think he made the best choice, but it's up to you mate, you could carry it on and make a further fool of him or call it a day."

"Fancy sharing a joint later?" John said. Garry just looked at him and smiled.

"Fancy a walk round the lake?" Garry said to John.

"Yeh, why not," he replied.

The lake was just behind 'B' dorm about two hundred yards from the fire door. It was about a hundred yards long and fifty yards wide with a small island in the centre joined by a narrow wooden bridge. On the other side of the lake was a large wooded area and beyond that lay the main road.

"Parcel run," Garry said, pointing to a path leading through the woods.

"By parcel run, I take it that's where late night parcels are left?"

"That's the place," Garry said. "Think there is a run tonight by your next door bed mate."

Lights had gone out and Garry, Andy and himself were sitting on chairs around his bed smoking the joint contributed by Terry. "Mike's out day after tomorrow," Andy said.

"Out?" John said.

"Yeh, that guy fourth row up on our side."

"Lucky bastard," Garry said. "Only one day to go."

Ten o'clock came and the same decent screw was walking up the dorm doing his night inspection. They just finished the joint they were smoking and Garry had thrown what was left out of the open window. "Evening lads," the screw said. All three of them said, "Evening."

"How's the hand, Davidson?"

"Fine thanks," John replied, surprised that he knew about his hand.

"Good," he said, as he walked away, and then stopped and turned to the three of them, with a smile on his face he said, "Lovely smell, night scented stock, surprised it's still in bloom this time of the year, good night." They all looked at each other.

"He fucking knows it's dope," Andy said. "What's he up to?"

Eleven thirty, Andy was standing by the fire door and one of the other lads at the bottom of the dorm watching the corridor. Andy was gone like a shot out across the fields to the other side of the lake, ten minutes later he still had not returned, John was by now in his bed and Garry had gone back to his. Twenty minutes later and Andy still had not come back. The door suddenly opened and in came Andy looking very pale, box in one hand and a screw handcuffed to the other. They both walked down the dorm and onto the corridor where another two screws were waiting; nobody had said anything during this period, they all just sat in their beds in silence.

When they had gone John got up and went over to Garry's bed. "Now what the fuck happens?" he said to Garry.

"Simple," he replied, "lock up in solitary for twenty-four hours then back to a closed nick to serve the rest of his sentence with a possible loss of some or all of his remission. Anyway, nothing we can do, so let's get some sleep." With that Garry pulled the sheets over him and John went back to his own bed with the sound of other voices around the dorm obviously talking about what had just transpired.

Chapter 10

John awoke about five thirty, not because of the lights being turned on but he was aware of someone moving around by the bed at the side of him. He sat up to see Andy and two screws; they were collecting all Andy's things out of his locker and stripping his bed. All the small items were put into a pillowcase he had taken off his pillow and all the bedding was under Andy's arms. Andy looked at John with a not so happy smile on his face, and said, "Nice to have met you mate, be good and hope your leg gets better," looking at the foot of his old bed.

Leg? John thought I have nothing wrong with my leg.

The screw looked at John and then Andy and with a sarcastic smirk said, "See you later you mean." John noticed it was the bastard who had escorted Terry back to the dorm after the trouble, "Still watching you," he said to John, and with that marched Andy out of the dorm and back to his twenty-three hour lock up and further degradation in a closed nick.

After breakfast, parade and the usual cleaning of the bed area it was back to education to show Grant what work they had done on the cycle shop project. They all worked as a team for the rest of the day pulling apart the shop and workshop plan that each of them had done and eventually they came to a mixture of all their plans and arrived at one very good plan. Grant looked pleased at the result and gave them another hour away from the work room anticipating that he would get the work completed faster if he gave them more space.

Nothing really happened during the rest of the day apart from doing more work on the project and them all agreeing to get the work completed as soon as possible in the hope that Grant would give them more free time. John had been to the library and got a nature book that had been illustrated by a guy called Orr which was full of the most fantastic ink drawings of animals and birds. John thought he would reproduce these on to A3 sheet card. He had always been good at this kind of drawing and could copy most things exactly.

He spent most of the evening working on a picture of a lion killing a gazelle, about eight o'clock he looked down the dorm to see a group of the guys around the fourth bed from the end, Mike's bed. What the fuck is going on, he thought to himself as he got up from the table to investigate? When he got to the men around the bed he noticed that all the bed sheets had been removed from the bed and Garry and some others were tying the sheets to the framework of the bed.

Garry came over to John and said, "Come on, give us a hand to get the end of the sheets over the roof frames."

"What's going on?" he said to Garry.

"Usual goodbye for Mike, always give them something to remember us by on their last night."

"So what happens now?" John asked.

"Well," Garry started, "we throw the ends of the bed sheets over the beams and all pull together to fasten his bed ten feet off the floor. One of the lads has taken Mike for a game of snooker until lights out."

"How does he get it back down?" John said.

"That's his problem," he said with a smile, "but if he has not managed it by four in the morning we normally help him so he can get at least one hour's sleep before his release at six."

"What about the screws?" asked John.

"They don't seem to notice," Garry said with a smile.

By eight thirty they were all back to what they were doing and John had gone back to his drawing, and the bed was secured to the ceiling of the dorm. Nine o'clock came and Mike came back to the dorm after his game of snooker. As he entered he stopped and looked up at the ceiling to see his bed, not exactly where he had left it. He looked around the dorm to see all the guys busy at what they were doing as if nothing had happened. "Come on," he said with a smile. "How the fuck am I going to get that down on my own?"

"WHAT?" one of the guys said with a look of innocence on his face, "nothing to do with us – like that when we came back from watching TV."

"Yeh," everyone said together.

"Must have been some of those bastards from 'C' dorm," another said.

Lights went dim at nine o'clock prompt. John and Garry went back to John's bed area to have a chat and have a smoke. Mike was still looking up at his bed scratching his head and working out how to get his bed down.

"Got any blow?" (dope) Garry said.

"No, run out last night."

"Bollocks," Garry said, "could just have done with one, always depresses me when someone is getting out. Brings it back to me the time I have still to serve."

"Yes," John said. "It has hit me like that the past hour or so." (He had been thinking a lot about his family while he had been drawing.) "HANG ON," he said to Garry. "Just had a thought," and with that got off his chair and went to the bed at the side of him, the bed that had been occupied by Andy. "Pick up the corner of the bed," he said to Garry.

Garry did as he was asked and John got down on his hands and knees, and pulled the rubber bung out of the leg of the bed. As he did so something dropped onto the floor out of the bed leg. John replaced the bung and picked up a block wrapped in cling film. John sat back down on his chair next to Garry and opened the small parcel.

"FUCK ME!" Garry said. "Blow."

That's what he was trying to tell me, John said to himself, that's what he meant when he said, hope your leg gets better.

The night screw turned into the dorm to do his normal inspection. As he got to Mike, who by now was sitting on the floor still looking up at his bed, he stopped looked at Mike and then up to the bed on the ceiling. "Going to emulate a bat are we?" he said with a smile, and continued his journey round the dorm without any further comment apart from the odd "evening" now and again.

John and Garry rolled a joint out of some of the blow that had been left for them by Andy, when suddenly there was a crash which made everyone in the dorm jump. All eyes turned to Mike's bed area to see Mike sitting on the roof cross section and half his bed on the floor. He had managed to climb onto the cross section and undo one of the sheets that fastened the bed to the ceiling, but underestimated the weight of the bed which plunged down onto the dorm floor almost taking Mike with it. He had decided that the only way to get the bed down was to throw caution to the wind and untie it. CRASH the rest of the bed came down as he untied the other end of the bed. With that he swung down off the beam onto the floor to the applause of all the guys on the dorm. He looked around and took a bow before pushing the bed back and remaking it.

John got up from his chair picking up one of the joints he had rolled for Garry and himself. He walked down the dorm to Mike's somewhat bent bed and handed him the joint. "Well done mate, didn't think you would manage it, best of luck for tomorrow, give my love to the outside world."

It was about five in the morning when John awoke bursting for a pee. He walked down the dorm towards the latrine when he noticed Mike was up and about collecting all his things and folding up his bedding. "OK?" John said to him, as he stopped by his now unmade bed.

"Fucking great," he replied. "Will be out with my wife and kids tonight for the first time in two years, feel ten feet tall."

"Last time in here?" John said to him.

"Sure is," he replied with a broad grin. "Just my wife and kids to concentrate on and getting a good job."

"Best of luck," John said as he continued his journey to have a pee.

Once more back at work and again Grant was going through the work carried out the previous day. It was about two when they had returned from lunch when one of the screws came into the office and went over to Grant and spoke to him and then turned and walked out. "Garry," he called out, "visitor for you." Garry's face lit up as he got up from his desk and walked towards the door. As he left John looked out of the window over the yard to the gatehouse and the visitors' block facing the car park. He saw Garry cross the yard and felt more than sad, that he had told Amy that she was never to visit him, but in his mind he still could not let his wife see him in the situation he was in or subject her to the humiliation of prison visits. As he looked across the car park he noticed a superb gold Rolls Royce with private number plates GR 4. Must pay the screws good money, he thought, to afford one of those, and assumed it was one of the prison hierarchy on a visit to the governor.

It was about an hour when Garry returned with a somewhat dismal look on his face. "OK?" John said to him as he sat down beside him.

"Yeh, always gets to me after a visit," he said.

"Well another good bit of work from you all," Grant said. "Only a bit more to do and your task will be completed."

Once more they were back at the dorm sitting around the table completing the final part of the cycle shop project, when John turned to Garry and asked him how his visit from his wife had gone.

"Good," he replied, he seemed to have shaken off the somewhat morose mood he had been in after his visit.

John decided it may be a good idea to change the subject of his wife's visit afraid it may send him back into a mood. "See we may have had a visit from one of the gods today," he said.

"Gods?" Garry replied.

"Yes, see the Rolls in the car park as you went past the one with the private plate?"

"Yes," he replied. "The one with GR 4, but not one of the gods as you put it, it's mine."

"YOURS?" John said with disbelief.

"Sure is," he said. John just looked at him. "Garry Reynolds," he said. "That's me."

"But how? Why?"

"Goes with the four hundred thousand pound house and the yacht in Spain," he smiled.

"Can I ask you?"

Garry stopped him. "Tell you tonight over a joint," he said. "Now let's go and eat."

They both sat down at their usual places to eat their evening meal when one of the guys from the next table came over to them. "Have you heard?" the man said.

"Heard?" John said. "Heard what?"

The man sat down in a vacant seat next to Garry. "Mike got a gate arrest this morning."

"You must be fucking joking," Garry said.

John looked first at the man and then at Garry. "What's a gate arrest?" John asked.

Garry explained that Mike had been arrested and taken into custody for another crime.

"But he had just done his time," John said.

"Yes, but it could be something in his past that he has done and they have only found out while he has been in here or the investigation has only been concluded while he has been banged up."

"He will be allowed home to see his family though won't he?" John asked.

"All depends what the charge is, could take him straight into custody."

John felt his stomach turn over. He should be out with his family tonight after two years apart, and now he could be in a nick somewhere, John thought.

Back at the dorm Garry and John were sitting round his bed smoking a joint Garry had bought from one of the dealers. John had to ask, "Does this happen much? This gate arrest I mean?"

"Happens now and again, and it's a bastard when it does, tends to fuck everyone's head up for a few days. Fancy a game of snooker for an hour?" Garry said.

"No thanks, couldn't concentrate," John said, knowing what Garry had meant about heads being fucked up.

Garry returned about an hour later to find John at the table putting the finishing touches to his drawing of the lion. "Fucking hell, that's good," Garry said. It was the third time in the last half hour that someone had come past the table and made the same remark.

"Thanks," John said. "It's almost finished."

"Are you going to do any more?" Garry said.

"I intend reproducing the complete book by the time I get out, he replied. "Fancy a brew?"

Garry said, "Sure, you make the brew and I'll go and skin up a few joints for later."

They sat around John's bed drinking tea and talking once more about Mike's gate arrest. John could not get it off his mind, putting himself in Mike's position.

"Look," Garry said, "let's put this conversation to bed, it's not doing anybody any good and creating nightmares."

"OK," John replied. "You were going to tell me about the Rolls," John said.

"Ah yes," Garry replied. "I wondered when we were going to get back to that."

"Look," John said, "it seems an unwritten rule that no one discusses what they are in for unless they volunteer to do so, so if..."

Garry stopped him. "No problem," Garry replied.

Garry started to tell John how it all started as an accident one night driving back from Nottingham when he stopped in a lay-by for a rest. In the lay-by was a flat topped wagon covered by a large green sheet, and Garry being Garry decided to see what was on the flat top. He got out of his car and went over to the trailer and undid one of the ropes securing the cover. As he pulled the cover back, he noticed the flat top was piled up with lengths of steel. Garry thought to himself, must be a fortune here. He then replaced the cover and thought nothing more about it until the following morning when he was returning to

Nottingham along the same road. As he approached the same lay-by he noticed the cab of a wagon turning into the lay-by and followed it in and took out his flask of tea. As he was having a drink, a guy got out of the cab and hooked up the trailer of steel and drove off, Garry looked at his watch nine o'clock, he had been in the lay-by at six o'clock the previous evening. That meant the steel had been left for fifteen hours.

Garry continued on his journey thinking how easy it would be to, for want of a better word 'remove' the steel in that time. He noticed a sign by the roadside advertising a transport café two hundred yards ahead. He pulled in and went inside to see most of the tables were taken up by truckers having their breakfast. He got himself a bacon sandwich and sat down at a table with one of the truckers who was having a full fry up. He started talking to the man about how bad the weather was and how it must be hard sleeping in the cab all night on a long haul. The man told Garry that most of the cabs like his did not have sleeping room and how they booked into a bed and breakfast or in his case, bed only. He told Garry how most of them without sleeping cabs would unhook the trailer in the nearest lay-by and just take the cab to wherever they would sleep for the night. BINGO, Garry had thought.

It was the weekend when he was having a drink in his local when he started talking to a guy he knew had done a bit of time for one thing and another, and then he brought up the price of scrap and processed metal. "Worth a few bob," his drinking pal said. He looked at Garry sensing that there was more than a passing interest in the matter. "Have you got some?" he asked Garry.

"Could have," Garry replied, "but it may be a bit moody if you understand my meaning."

"Let's sit down," he said to Garry. "Want to tell me?" he said to Garry when they had sat down.

Garry told him that he could get tons of the stuff but required a wagon cab with trailer pick up facilities and an outlet that would not ask questions and pay cash. The man with Garry whose name turned out to be Phil, said, "Can you leave it with me?"

"Sure," Garry said. "Think you can sort it out?"

"Don't know, but are you in here next Friday?"

"Can be," Garry replied.

"Good will be in about eight," and with that finished his drink and said, "see you Friday."

"I'm starting to get the picture very clear," John said to Garry as they lit up a second joint.

"Well, I don't think I have to say much more then," he smiled at John.

"No, no, go on," John said intrigued by his story.

"OK," Garry said, "but you aren't stupid so I will make it short."

"The following Friday I met Phil in the pub and he said he had sorted it but what was in it for him. I asked him what he had. He told me he could borrow a cab and had seen a metal merchant who would pay cash at the right price. I told him that if he drove the cab I would follow in the car and I would go fifty-fifty with him, which he agreed, and that's the story," he said to John.

"Bloody hell, but where does the Rolls and the house and yacht come in?"

Garry smiled. "Out of the four point five million over four years."

John could feel his jaw drop, "Four point five MILLION, fuck me, I don't want to ask," John said. "But how many life sentences have you got for that?"

"Eighteen months."

"Eighteen fucking months?" John repeated.

"Yeh, could only prove three thousand pounds, as all the proof had been shipped abroad ages ago and the metal dealer was not going to tell them as he had been done for receiving and there is a bit of a difference between receiving four mill, and three thousand," he smiled at John and said, "well I have shown you mine so to speak, what's your story?"

John told him his story a little embarrassed at how boring it was compared to Garry's. After he had finished which took about two minutes to tell. Garry said, "That's a bastard. I've done what you did three times and had no problems, YET."

Chapter 11

The following morning the same old ritual and the completion day for their cycle shop project. They worked hard to complete the full set up of the shop from banking projected figures to sales staff and marketing. Grant seemed a bit nervous today and pushed for completion by the end of the day, even asking them to only take half an hour for lunch instead of one hour. Normally, they would have told any screw, civvy or otherwise to get fucked, but after all he had given them plenty of time off so they all agreed.

John and Garry sat eating their evening meal and the question of Grant came up. "Don't you think he looked a little uptight today?" John asked.

"Sure did, maybe he is under pressure from that head of department, what's his name?"

"McKay," John replied.

"Yes that's it," Garry said, "nasty bastard that."

Back at the dorm John decided to start another drawing out of the book illustrated by Orr. Garry had decided to go for a walk round the lake and call in at the library. He had just started work on the picture when a man sat facing him at the table. "Can you do cards?" he said to John.

John looked up at the man, "CARDS?"

"Yeh cards, as in birthday cards."

"Well yes I suppose so."

"You see it's my wife's birthday next week and it would be great if I could send her one."

"Why have you come to me?" John said.

"One of the guys in 'C' dorm has seen your drawings and I thought if you could do that kind of work you may be able to do cards."

"What's it worth?" John asked, he had found out in nick nothing was for nothing.

"An eighth of blow?"

"OK, come back on Sunday."

"Cheers," the man said and walked off back out of the dorm.

He continued with his drawing until Garry came back to the dorm. "Brew?" he said to John.

"Cheers," John replied. Five minutes later he was back at the table with two mugs of hot tea, with no milk, they were always running out of their allocation of dried milk.

Garry sat down, and said, "Just had a word with one of the lads from 'E' dorm, got a new guy in today, in for car theft."

"So what's new?"

"The thing is a screw has grassed him up and it appears that he is a nonce case, been shagging his own daughter."

"Fuck me, "John said. "So they have given him a false rap sheet?"

"Always the same," Garry said, "thing is even the screws have a downer on them and things tend to SLIP out and eyes don't see anything. Well it's 'E' dorm's problem, sit back and watch this space so to speak."

John worked on his new drawing until lights out and decided on an early night. It had been late nights all week and he was feeling a little drained. His night was a restless one made up of dreams of Amy and the children mixed up with gate arrests. When he woke up at five thirty he was glad to escape the monsters of his dreams and went to have a shower and get dressed. As he was early he decided to clean around his bed area to save doing it after parade. He had just finished when Garry came over to him, "Early bird?" he said to John.

"Yeh, bad night," he replied.

"Gate arrest?" Garry said.

"How the fuck did you know?"

"Told you it fucks the mind up," he said with a smile.

They both went to have breakfast and noticed three tables down there was a man sitting on his own. This was a table that most of the men from 'E' dorm used. Garry looked at John and winked, "That's our car thief," he said as they sat down to eat their breakfast.

Suddenly there was a crash, and they both looked in the direction of where the noise came from to see one of the guys from 'E' dorm had tripped up and spilt hot tea over the head of the man sitting on his own. The man shouted in pain, the man who had spilt the tea turned round to get another one, the screw nearest looked out of the window.

"Come on let's go and find out what is the next project that we have to do."

"Hope it's not back to fucking computers," John said.

As they walked into the education room they were confronted by McKay and a woman of about thirty-five, not beautiful but very attractive stood at the side of him. McKay looked at them as they walked in with the usual look of distaste. "Sit," he said. As they took their seat he said, "This is Norma Finley, she is your new tutor. You will all do as you are instructed, any breach of rules or pissing about will be reported to me. I am sure you all understand," and with that walked out of the room.

She looked at them all with a smile on her face and said, "As Mr McKay said, I'm Norma Finley, you guys call me Norma, at least to my face," she said with an even broader smile. "Perhaps you would like to stand up in turn and introduce yourselves. I have your profile records which I have read and found quite impressive. All I would like to do now is put a face to the names."

Each of the guys did as instructed and sat back down. "Right before we go onto what we will be doing are there any questions?"

"Yes, I have one," John said.

"What's that John?" she said.

"What has happened to Grant?"

"Oh, I take it he didn't tell you, well he decided he wanted a change in direction and is going to open a cycle sales and repair business," they all looked at each other.

"The crafty bastard," said Garry out loud.

Norma stood in front of them all and started to go through a list of the forthcoming work. John was pleased to notice there was no mention of computer programming. "You all have skills in a broad range of things and what I am going to do is to match those skills with the various tasks as they come up. The first things I have printed out for you all to look at. I want you all to look at the list and choose what you would like to get involved in," with that she handed a sheet of paper to each of them.

John looked down the list of projects which included, interview techniques, office management, computer skills and many more. At the top of the paper was a section to put your name and beside each subject was a box to tick for anything you would like to do.

"I will be tea lady for today, and you look through and complete the form before lunch." With that she went into the tea room after asking who took sugar.

Garry looked at John, smiled and said, "She sounds fine." John nodded in agreement.

They all handed the completed forms back to Norma who spent a short while looking through them; she looked up obviously pleased at the result. "Well," she said, "you all seem to know your own strengths and weaknesses. I notice you have all put down computer studies, apart from you John," she said looking at him.

"Yes," he said, "if you have a course on Mandarin Chinese I would understand that better, and go for that."

She smiled and said, "According to your file you will not be in here long enough to complete that."

"I'm a quick learner," he said with a wink of his eye.

She smiled and said, "I'm sure you are but we are talking about an education programme." The rest of the guys laughed at the innuendo.

"So am I," he said with another wink.

"I'm getting off this road," she said with a smile. "OK, as it so happens you all fit in with the tasks ahead. There is one project which is not on the project sheet, and that is a debate on prison reform. We have been approached by the BBC to make an internal documentary conducted by inmates. What this means is that we are to select a number of inmates to discuss how prison could be changed for the benefit of the offender and society, this would be chaired by an inmate from the education department."

They all looked at her not knowing what to say.

"Well after looking at your history profiles I have a good idea who would fit well into this roll, but I must ask for a show of hands. Anybody who would like to be considered to be a film star?" she said with a grin. As they all looked around the room no hands went up. "Good," she said, "that makes my job a little easier. John, having looked through your file, I see you have been involved in conducting seminars and sales debates."

"Oh no," John said.

"Oh yes," Norma replied with a smile. "YOU'RE IT."

Garry and John sat in the canteen having lunch, when Garry turned to John with a huge smile on his face and said, "Will you do something for me?"

"Yes, what?"

"Will you sign my autograph book when we get back to the dorm?"

"FUCK OFF," John said.

Back at the education office Norma handed them a pack of papers relating to the B.E.C. course on office management, asking questions that related to personnel management and staff training – things like if someone was less experienced than you was promoted over you how would you react? And what would you do if you found out that your office manager was fucking your secretary?

"Could I ask you to complete the first four pages by tomorrow?" Norma said. "You can start it now but if it is not completed by the time we finish today could you complete it by tomorrow morning?"

They worked on the question paper until Norma said, "Well guys time to go," as she put on her coat. "Oh by the way John, I need to spend the first hour with you to go through the forthcoming BBC thing."

"Sure," John said, "see you tomorrow."

Garry looked at him trying to suppress a laugh. "Go on give her a kiss good night."

"FUCK OFF," he said. "I don't think you're funny."

A few minutes later he was back at the dorm after first collecting a letter from Amy. He was sat by his bed when Garry came over with two cups of tea and a joint. "Cheers," John said putting the letter down on top of his locker.

"Been down to 'E' dorm to see one of the lads," Garry said. "They were having a bit of fun with the nonce case. Apparently the guy wears a wig and while he was in the shower they had nicked it and they had put it into the drawer of his locker – managed to turn the drawer upside down without anything falling out and put four six inch nails through it. Fuck knows how he will be able to get it open and when he does everything is going to fall out all over the floor."

John laughed, "Serves the bastard right."

"I think they have something else to piss him off big style," Garry said.

"What's that?" John said.

"Don't know, but they reckon he won't be in here after it kicks off."

They finished their meal in the canteen and decided to go for a walk round the lake. As they got close, John noticed that the lake had about nine or ten ducks on it, that had not been there the last time they had been round the lake. "Long time since I have had duck," John said.

"Me too," Garry responded, "used to have it once a week." John looked at Garry with a smile on his face, "FORGET IT," Garry said.

"What?"

"You know what, we couldn't cook it anyway."

"Suppose not," John replied as they continued round the lake.

They sat in the TV room watching a film about some wartime adventure when Garry turned to John and said, "I'm pissed off with this. Let's have a game of snooker." As they got to the games room all the tables were being used and two guys were waiting, one of whom was Terry. Shortly a table came free and Terry and the other man went over to it to set up the balls. When they had done this, John noticed Terry saying something to the other man, and they both looked over to Garry and himself. John got a tight grip on the snooker cue as Terry walked towards them. "Fancy a game of doubles?"

"Yeh why not," Garry said rather surprised, as he expected a bit of trouble with Terry having a back-up man behind him. They went over to the table and the other man said, "What we playin for?"

"What do you want to play for?" John asked.

"An eighth of smoke?" the man replied. John looked at Garry who was nodding his head in approval.

Terry broke off and Garry followed with a thirteen break. The game went on for about half an hour with Terry and his partner obviously out classed by John and Garry.

"Well that gave us a good kicking," Terry said with a smile which showed a gap in his teeth. "Come over later," Terry said, "and bring the smoke."

"OK don't forget," Garry said as they turned and walked out of the room.

As they sat round John's bed having a smoke and drinking some alcoholic brew which Garry had acquired from somewhere, Terry came to the side of the bed and threw two small packs on the bed. "One for me and one from Pete." He must be the guy he was playing with, John thought.

"Cheers," they both said at the same time as they picked up their prize. Terry hovered around and John felt that he would like to ask him to join them, but was afraid of the answer.

John looked at Garry and gave a slight nod, Garry must have thought the same and nodded back to John, "Got any blow?" John said to the man still hovering around.

"Yeh, got two joints," he said, as he reached into his shirt pocket.

"Want a drink?" John said as he pulled up a chair for Terry to sit on.

"Yeh, thanks," as he put the two roll-ups on the bed. Garry passed him the mug with the unnamed liquid in, as John picked up the two joints. He had got into the nothing for nothing syndrome very well during the past few weeks.

The night inspection had come and gone and Garry had gone back to his bed, after a combination of booze and dope he had suddenly gone down hill rapidly.

"Don't want to make too much of it," Terry suddenly said, "but where the fuck did you come from the other day? I mean one minute I was stood there and the next thing I was on the floor with half my fucking head missing."

John knew it was only a matter of time before the fight came up. "LUCK," John said.

"Like fuck," he said with a smile holding his hand out to John.

The following morning John woke up as the lights went on feeling a little bit the worse for wear and went for a shower and got dressed. After breakfast which Terry joined them for, it was back to education, and John's talk with Norma about the forthcoming BBC documentary. All the other guys started on the project that Norma had given them the previous day. He sat down at her desk to be given a sheet of paper with questions to be asked at the debate. What do you think? How would you change things? And many more direct questions which he was not quite sure what the response would be under a filming situation. There was also a list of names of the inmates who had either volunteered or been instructed to take part.

"When is this going to take place?" John asked.

"Next Friday," she replied, "in the large hall down the corridor."

"Didn't know we had a large hall," John said.

"Come on I'll show it to you," she said, as she got up from her chair.

Garry overheard the last few words, smiling he said, "What is Norma going to show you?" he said with a wink, John turned to him with one finger in the air.

They walked down the corridor and through a set of double doors and into a large room with a stage at the far end; the rest of the room was empty apart from tables and chairs piled up around the room. Norma showed him a sheet of paper with a floor plan drawn out. "This is how the seating is to be arranged," she said as she laid it out on one of the tables. "You will be sat here," as she pointed to the drawing, "and all the participants will be sat around these tables," again pointing to the floor plan. "If you have any ideas about how it could be changed let me know, but remember the camera and lighting is to be set up here," again pointing to the sheet of paper. "Take this back with you tonight and if you have any ideas, let me know tomorrow."

The rest of the day they all spent on the B.E.C. papers, only interrupted by lunch. During lunch John said, "DUCK."

Garry looked at John and said, "Duck?"

"Yes the duck."

"What fucking duck?"

"The ducks on the lake. I was thinking, we can cook a duck."

"And where do you suppose to cook this fucking duck?" Garry said with a questioned look on his face.

"The tea boiler in the dorm boiler room."

"The boiler?"

"Yep," John replied. "We pluck it, put it in the boiler for an hour and hey presto, one boiled duck."

"You have finally lost the plot my son," Garry said. "If you put a duck in the boiler you would get all the water full of grease."

"Yep thought of that, the last thing we want is for all the lads' tea to have grease floating on top, but why use OUR boiler?"

"Oh no," Garry said, "you will get us hung."

"Not if nobody finds out who did it," John said with a smile. Garry just shook his head as they set off back to education.

Once more they got back to their task until it was time for them to finish for the day but not before John had raided the stationery cupboard for more pens and sheets of paper.

On the way back to the dorm John stopped outside the nick shop and asked Garry to wait for him. A couple of minutes later he came out holding a golf club.

"What the fuck is that?" Garry asked.

"A three iron," he replied, "noticed last week that one was in the shop behind the cage, and asked the screw what it was for.

He told me he kept it there with a few balls in case anyone wanted to use it on the field at the back of the dorms."

"I didn't know you played golf?" Garry said.

"I don't," John replied with a smile. Garry just shook his head.

They finished their evening meal and set off back to the dorm. John to complete the birthday card for the guy who had come into the dorm a few days before. He completed after about an hour drawing flowers and teddy bears and things like that and making an envelope secured by glue – another gift from education. He walked over to Garry's bed holding the golf club. "Fancy a game of golf?" he said to the man lying on his bed.

Garry looked up at him and then out of the window. "It's nearly dark," he said to John.

"Best time," John replied. "Come on."

They walked through the fire doors at the end of the dorm and across the field leading to the lake. "What ARE you doing?" Garry said, "and where are the balls?"

"Don't need any," John said smiling as he walked closer to the lake side. All the ducks had come off the water and were sitting on the bank with their heads tucked under their wings. Garry just looked at him knowing by now where this game of golf was heading. Slowly John walked up to one of the sleeping birds and gave a little tap on its back. As it removed its head from under its wing and looked round, John took a swing that Tiger Woods would have been proud of. 'Whack' the club caught the duck on the back of its head; it didn't even have time to quack. John bent down and picked up the dead duck and looked at Garry, smiled and said, "Got any orange sauce?"

Back at the dorm, John put the duck in his locker, by now it had been plucked and cleaned and wrapped in a piece of cling film acquired from the kitchen. They both sat down by John's bed smoking a joint. "Now what are you going to do with it?" Garry said, still not believing what had just happened.

"Wait and see." They sat around the bed for about an hour and then John went round to his locker and took the duck out. "Come on," he said to Garry. "Let's go cooking."

Garry looked a bit apprehensive but followed him out of the dorm and over to 'C' dorm.

"You keep watch," he said to Garry as he went into the dorm boiler room, took the top off the large container and placed the duck in the boiling water. Having replaced the boiler lid they crept out and back to their dorm to wait an hour or so before they would return and retrieve their supper.

An hour and a half later they were on their way back to 'C' dorm with Garry keeping watch while John crept back into the boiler room and collected the duck. John had found a carrier bag and put the duck inside.

As they returned to their own dorm Terry was at the entrance. "Fancy a drop of scotch?" he said to them both, "managed to swap a quarter of blow for some with a guy out of the kitchen."

"Sure do," Garry replied, "fancy some duck?"

"DUCK?" Terry replied. "Where the fuck have you got a duck from?"

"Flew in through the open window," John said, with a wink at Garry.

It was about eleven o'clock. The night-time screw had been and gone after his night inspection and the three of them were sitting round John's bed, eating the duck having a joint and drinking the whiskey out of a plastic cup.

"Big drop tomorrow," Terry said.

"Whereabouts?" Garry said.

"Same place as Andy got a pull, in the woods."

"Who's the runner?" John asked.

"Got no one," Terry replied. "Guys are too nervous about the pull on the last one. The man is offering half a block of blow to whoever does it."

"Fuck me," John said. "That's a lot of blow." He looked at Garry.

"No fucking way," Garry said.

"Look," John said, "the screws all know that we know about the pull and where it was. What's the chance of them doing a check on the same area?"

"I don't know," Garry said, "but they may think the same as you."

"Only thing is Terry said it's a two man job due to the amount."

John looked at Garry with raised eyebrows. "Watch my lips," Garry said, "FUCK OFF."

"Half a block, that's a big lump." John said. "When is the drop?" John asked Terry.

"Tomorrow at eleven."

John looked at Terry and said, "Tell your man it's three quarters and a full scotch."

Garry looked at John, and said, "NO WAY you crazy bastard."

Chapter 12

It was five to eleven the following night and John and Garry were sitting on John's bed. "What the fuck are we doing?" Garry said.

"Going walkies," John replied as he got off the bed and headed to the fire door. Garry followed him looking back to see Terry taking his place by the entrance to the dorm.

It was a cold night and they could see their breath in the cold night air. They both ran off in the direction of the lake looking round to see any movement or glare of a torch. They got to the side of the lake, and four or five ducks rose noisily into the air frightening the shit out of both of them. Round the lake and into the woods looking for the fence and the large rock where they had been told the parcel would be left. They got to a large oak tree and stopped to get their breath. "Where the fuck is it?" Garry whispered to John.

"Let's try over there," he said, and with that set off in the direction of the perimeter fence. They had gone about fifty yards when Garry said, "There that's the rock." As they approached they noticed two large boxes by the side of the rock, they went over and picked them up. "Right let's get back rapid." Five minutes later they were going back through the fire doors and into the dorm. Once inside they went down the dorm to the boiler room and put the boxes down on the floor. "Fuck me we did it," Garry said. "Let's get back to our beds and leave the rest to Terry."

"You go," John said, "will be with you in a minute."

Garry left the room and went back to his bed followed by John about two minutes later. They sat on Garry's bed still panting from their run. Garry had a bit of a shake on him that John put down to nerves, as he himself had a bit of the shakes.

"Let's get to bed," John said as he got off Garry's bed and headed back to his.

The following morning Garry came over to John's bed just as he was getting up. "Well what a fucking night that was," Garry said. "But never thought about it, when will we get our split?" John smiled, and went to his locker and took out a bottle of scotch and a full block of blow. "That's why you stayed behind," Garry said.

"Yep, trust no fucker," John replied.

"Hang on, Garry said, "that's a full block."

"Yeh."

"But the deal was a three quarter."

"Yeh, as I said, can't trust anybody in here can you? The drop guy must have had a quarter away don't you think?"

"You are going to get us hung," Garry said with a broad grin.

After they had got dressed they went to the canteen for breakfast. "Well nice to have Saturday here and no education for two days," John said. Just then the man who had ordered the birthday card came over to them to check the card would be finished for tomorrow. "All done," John said, "ready for you to pick up later."

"Cheers," the man said as he sat down on a chair next to Garry, "heard about wiggy the nonce?" he asked.

"No, what about him?"

The man continued, "He's in the infirmary."

"Why what's happened?" John said.

"Well last night about eleven someone set fire to his wig."

"His fucking wig?" John laughed.

"Yeh and it's burnt his head."

"Why didn't he take it off?" Garry said.

"Couldn't," the man replied, "one of the guys had got hold of some super glue and stuck it to his head." John burst out laughing. "I'm surprised you didn't hear all the fuss the screws were making running up and down the corridor."

"What time was this?" John asked.

"About ten past eleven," the man replied.

Garry looked at John with a smile and said, "Thanks wiggy."

When they arrived back at the dorm they noticed the empty bed that had been vacated by one of the guys who had been released two days before after being tied to a chair and left on the corridor for the screws to find, had a new guy making up the bed. He was an old guy about seventy years of age. John went up to him and said, "OK young man, just joined our happy band?"

"Yes, the man replied as he held out his hand and said, "George."

"My name's John and this is Garry," as he took his hand.

"Nice to be back with the boys," George said with a smile.

"Back?" Garry said.

"Yes, been out for two weeks, nobody I know on the outside and with winter here and Christmas coming up I'm better off inside."

John and Garry looked at each other, John said, "You are GLAD to be banged up?"

"Yes," the man said. "Been in nick for most of my life," he said, "nothing for me on the outside. I'm sixty-nine and since I was nineteen, spent thirty-five years in and out of prison. Got released two weeks ago and lived in a hostel, no mates, no family, no home and no leg," he said as he rolled up his right trouser leg. John and Garry looked down to see the man had a false leg.

"Fancy a brew?" Garry said to him as he walked off to his locker.

"Please," George said.

They sat round the old man's bed drinking the tea Garry had made and listening to the old man's story. "How come you got sent down this time?" John asked."

"Well as I said I was out for two weeks and totally pissed off, so I threw a brick through a shop window, and stood there waiting for the old bill to turn up along with the man who owned the shop, so they arrested me and I ended up in court yesterday. The judge who I had been up before had a social worker report and gave me a three hour sentence, and told me I would serve it sat at the back of the court room. Well that was no good for me, so I told him to fuck off and threw my walking stick at the clerk of the court, so he had no alternative but to give me three months for contempt of court," he said with a smile. John and Garry just looked at each other not knowing what to say. "Well," he said, "time for a kip," as he lay down on his bed and closed his eyes.

"See you later," John said as he got up to leave the smiling old man to his happy sleep.

John worked on some more of his drawings for the rest of the day and Garry went to watch some TV. Later on a voice at the bottom of his bed said, "John, got a message from the office, you've got a visit on Monday at ten." John looked up to see Barry the blue band.

"A visit?" I don't have visits," he said.

"You do now, something to do with the personnel department from the company you worked for. The company, he thought what the fuck could that be about? He was lying on his bed thinking about his visit when the man he had done the birthday card came up to him.

"OK if I have my card?" he said.

"OK if I have my blow," John replied. The man reached in his pocket and brought out a small package and put it on his bed. John got the card out of his locker and handed it to the man.

"Fucking hell that's good," he said with a smile. John had even decorated the envelope with garlands of flowers. "Thanks a lot," he said as he took the card and walked back down the dorm.

Barry stood at the bottom of the dorm and shouted for them all to listen. "Governor's inspection ten o'clock tomorrow," he said, "so all bed areas are to be one hundred percent clean, beds made up and all of you clean shaven and full inspection dress including ties. Stand by your beds with hands by your side, do NOT speak unless you are asked to do so. If so you will address him as sir, OK guys?" They all nodded in agreement.

Ten o'clock came the following day and they were all lined up as instructed. John had noticed that George the old man was having trouble putting his false leg on and time was getting on for the inspection. He went over to the old man when he had finished cleaning his bed area and cleaned around his bed while another of the guys had polished his bed frame and made his bed for him. John could understand why George liked it in here.

The governor walked into the dorm spot on ten o'clock accompanied by a senior prison officer. He walked past all the men stopping now and again to say something to some of the men. As he got to John he looked at the wall at the back of his bed, which John had hung some of his drawings. "You do those?" he said to John.

"Yes sir," he replied.

"Was that your job on the outside or just a hobby?"

"Just a hobby sir," he again replied.

"They are very, very good," he said.

"Thank you," John replied. "Would you like me to do one for you?" he said. This was met by a scowl from the screw at the side of him.

The governor looked at him and with a smile said, "Maybe, maybe," as he continued on his inspection.

The rest of the day went by with John doing more artwork and him writing another letter to Amy. He still kept thinking about his visit tomorrow but still could not work out why someone from his company was coming to see him.

Over their evening meal, one of the guys from 'C' dorm asked John if they had any trouble with the water in the boiler being greasy.

"Funny you should say that," John replied. "I only said to Garry this morning that the tea tasted a little greasy, didn't I?" turning to Garry with a smile.

"Yes you did," Garry lied.

Monday arrived and they were all sitting at their desks in education, when one of the screws came in and said, "Davidson, visitor." John got up and followed the man outside and across the yard to the visitors' block. It was the first time he had been in there. It was not as big as he thought it would be, it had rows of tables with chairs either side. At one of the tables sat a woman of about fifty dressed in a smart grey suit. The screw pointed to her and said, "Over there, Davidson."

John went over to the table and the woman stood up to greet him. She held out her hand he took hold of it as she said, "Hello John my name's Mary Johnson from the personnel department, shall we sit down?"

"Sure," John said and sat down facing her.

"I suppose you are wondering what this is all about," she said with a smile.

"Well, I most certainly am," John replied, returning her smile.

"Right I'll start off by telling you the company policy on people with a criminal record, that is due to circumstances within the company which I can't go into, but basically dependant upon the offence it does not mean that the company will not close the door on you. Now as I understand you were found guilty of obtaining a mortgage by fraud, is that correct?"

"Yes," he replied.

"We have had a meeting at the office and decided that on your release we want to see you with a possible job offer. Now this job may not be in the same position as you have had but at least it will give you employment with a chance to develop within the company." She stopped and looked at John waiting for his response.

"I don't know what to say," he said to her, "that was the last thing I expected, but I can't understand why."

"Well all I can say, we can all make mistakes, even directors of companies," she replied with a bit of a wink. John got the feeling she was trying to tell him something without actually telling him anything. She got up from the table saying, "Have got to go now John, when you get out give me a call and we will arrange a meeting."

She held out her hand and he took it saying, "Thanks a lot, will call you as soon as I can." With that she turned and walked out of the room past the screw at the door.

John walked back into education with a beaming smile on his face. He sat down at his desk next to Garry, as Garry looked at him and said, "You look a happy bunny."

"Sure am," he replied. "Tell you at dinner time."

They sat down to eat their dinner and Garry turned to John and said, "Well?"

John started to tell him about his meeting with Mary and the fact that he stood a good chance of a job when he got out.

"That's fucking great," Garry said, "but what I can't understand is why?"

"Reading between the lines I think one of the top guys in the company has been a bad boy at some time and has not forgotten, and is willing to give people another chance."

Garry repeated himself, "Fucking great."

The rest of the day went as normal in education, filling in forms, taking a few tests and John going through the question sheets for the forthcoming B.B.C. documentary. Soon the day was over and they were all headed back to their dorms.

As they turned into their dorm Barry the blue band was standing by the door of his room. They both said 'hi' to him as they approached, he returned the acknowledgement and held his hand up to stop them both.

"What's up?" John said.

"You will see when you go into the dorm," he said. "It seems we have inherited a fucking nut case, come on I will show you." They walked into the dorm, as he entered he looked up at the ceiling, and there on one of the horizontal beams sat a small thin guy. He looked down at them and with a big smile said, "Hi guys."

John and Garry looked at each other and then at Barry, "Who the fuck is that?" John asked.

Barry inclined his head to tell them both to follow him; they went into Barry's room and sat down on the chairs by his table. "That is Mark."

"What the fuck is he doing up there?" Garry asked.

"Apparently he spends all his free time up there, that is when he is not swinging from one beam to the other," Barry replied.

"Where did he come from?" John said.

"Well this is the story. Apparently he is inside for cat burglary. He has been transferred from 'E' dorm where he has driven them fucking mad over the past few weeks and got himself in a bit of trouble, so they made a swap with one of our guys, thinking it may calm him down and stop someone in 'E' dorm punching his lights out. He can fucking climb ANYTHING better than a monkey," Barry said.

"And what the fuck are we going to do with him?" John asked.

"Well one of the screws knows about the trouble you had with Terry, and in his wisdom thought that between you," pointing to John, "and Terry, you may be able to persuade him to be a good boy and not to act like fucking Tarzan."

"Oh yes, and if we sort him out, me and Terry get into trouble," John said.

Barry looked at John and said, "Certain eyes will be closed if you get my drift as long it is not too rough. The thing is the screws can't watch him all the time and at the end of the day there is no ruling about someone wanting to sit in the roof where he is doing no harm."

"Leave it with me," John said as he and Garry got up to leave. As they walked out of the blue band's room Terry was coming into the dorm. "Ah, just the man, come with me," John said.

They walked into the dorm and Terry looked up at the man on the beam, he looked at John and said, "Who the…"

John stopped him, "Tell you back at my pitch," as he continued up the dorm to his bed area. The three of them sat around his bed and John told Terry all that Barry had told him.

"Well what the fuck can we to do about it?" Terry asked.

"Well for the time being, just let's play it by ear," John replied.

"One question I find hard," Terry said.

"What's that?" John asked.

"Barry said he swings from beam to beam."

"Yes," John replied, "look at those beams, they are over seven feet apart, no one can swing that distance, apparently HE can," John said looking at the man in the roof going from beam to beam.

Terry and Garry turned to look down the dorm. "Fuck me," they both said together.

They stayed around John's bed drinking tea and having a smoke until it was time to eat. Mark was still sitting on one of the beams. They went together for their evening meal wondering who was going to serve a meal to the nutcase on the beams. As they sat down the monkey walked into the canteen got his food and walked over to them. "Mind if I sit here?" he said to them.

"No sit down, we need to have a bit of a talk."

"Thanks," he said as he took a seat. "My name's Mark."

"Yes we know," John replied, "we believe you had a bit of trouble in your last dorm?"

"Yep," he replied. "Guys took a dislike to me just because I like to be in the air."

Terry turned to him and said, "Tell me WHY do you like to be in the air?"

"Don't know just do," he replied.

"Well in 'B' dorm I would suggest you find a more conventional way of getting round. Some of us are in the education department and have to concentrate on our work in our free time which is hard enough without being distracted by someone swinging about over our fucking heads."

"They said that in the other dorm," he replied with a strange smile.

They left the nutcase at the table to finish his meal and made their way back to the dorm, John got on with another drawing and Garry and Terry went to the games room. About ten minutes later Mark came into the dorm, stood on his bed and swung himself onto one of the beams, and there he stayed until Garry and Terry came back just before lights out. They came over to John and Terry said, "How long has he been up there?"

"Since he came back from the canteen," John replied shaking his head. "Fancy a drink tonight after the screw has done his inspection?" John asked.

"Sure," Terry said. "I'll bring a bit of blow over."

An hour and a half later they were sitting round John's bed sharing a drink out of one cup and passing round a joint. John looked down the dorm to see a figure swinging towards them; he quickly put the cup under the bed just as the man appeared above their heads.

"Hi," the nutcase said, looking down from his perch.

"Fuck off," Terry said.

"That's not nice," the man said. Terry jumped on John's bed to get hold of one of the man's leg, but before he had managed to get to him the guy had swung to another beam. "Want to play do you?" the man said.

"Yeh, I want to play," replied Terry

"Get down off the bed," John said to Terry, "he's just taking the piss."

"Taking the piss? I'll kick the piss out of him when he comes down."

"Yes, you do that, he screams screw and you end up on a charge." They finished their drink about midnight and decided to settle down for the night. Mark was still on one of the beams.

Chapter 13

The following morning John was on his way to the washroom and noticed Mark's bed had been slept in but there was no sign of him. As he entered he saw him at one of the washbasins talking to Terry. He went over to them to hear the nutcase say to Terry. "Yeh two of the other guys in the other dorm did that and now they are back in a lock up nick with loss of time, so carry on," he said again with that weird smile.

John just managed to grab Terry's arm as he went to punch the man in the face. "Leave it," he instructed Terry as he pulled him away from the nutcase.

Terry looked at John and said, "I'll fucking kill that bastard." The man smiled at them both and walked out of the room.

At the end of another day John and Garry got back to the dorm to find Terry on his hands and knees by Mark's bed. They went over to him and noticed he had a hacksaw in his hand. "What the fuck are you doing?" John said.

"Fixing that little twat," he replied. They noticed Terry had all but cut through the frame of one side of the bed and had started on the other side. "Just wait till the bastard sits on his bed, let alone tries to sleep on it." He finished his task and remade the bed, then went out of the dorm to replace the saw back in the workshop.

He returned about ten minutes later and came over to John and Garry who were sitting by John's bed. "Right let's sit back and watch the fun."

About ten minutes later Mark came into the dorm and went over to his bed, he looked down the dorm at the three of them and put on that weird smile.

"Yes, smile you bastard," Terry said, go and have your swing."

John said, "Swing? I think his bed is his problem."

Terry looked at John, and said, "Don't you believe it."

"Why? What the fuck have you done?"

"Just watch," he said with a smile.

Mark sat down on his bed and the next thing was BANG, he was on the floor with the bed in two pieces either side of him. All three looked down the dorm to notice he wasn't smiling anymore. He got off the floor and marched out in the direction of the blue band's room. A short while later he returned accompanied by Barry. He was talking to him and pointing up the dorm towards the three of them around John's bed.

Barry started to walk up the dorm towards them with Mark at his side, as they got to them, Terry said, "What happened there?"

"You fucking know what happened," the nutcase said.

"ME? How the fuck can I know? We were sat having a smoke and the next thing you were on the floor."

"You cut my fucking bed in half," he said.

"Not me," Terry replied.

"Must have been rust," Garry replied with a smile.

"Belt up," Barry said. He turned to a very irate Mark, "You go back to bed while I sort this out."

"Half a bed," Terry piped up with a broad grin. The owner of half a bed stormed back down the dorm.

Barry looked at the three of them with half a smile. "Who did it?" he said.

"Not us," Terry said.

"No, as we came in the dorm we saw someone leaving," said John.

"What was he like?" Barry asked with a knowing smile.

They all looked at each other and Garry said, "He was a small guy, yeh, about six foot five."

Terry said, "And very thin, yes, about nineteen stone."

Barry interjected, "OK, OK I get the drift."

"Get your story right. I will have to let the screws know, but will tell the one who suggested Mark's transfer to the dorm. I am sure he will understand," he said with a wink as he set off back down the dorm.

"I think Tarzan is a little pissed off," John said.

"Pissed off? He doesn't know what pissed off is yet," Terry said with a knowing look on his face.

About half an hour later, Barry was at the bottom of the dorm with a screw at his side. Barry pointed over to what was left of Mark's bed and they both walked over to it. He started talking to the screw and at the same time pointing up the dorm to the three of them sitting around John's bed. After a short while the screw and Barry were standing in front of them. "I understand from your blue band that you saw someone not from this dorm walking out as you arrived back today, is that correct?"

"Yes sir," John said.

"What was he like?" the screw replied.

Terry said, "We couldn't see too well, we came through the fire door as he was going out onto the corridor."

The screw looked at Barry and said, "All I can do is to put it down on my report that this was done by person or persons unknown."

"Yes sir," Barry replied looking at the three of them. Barry stood at the bottom of the dorm. "I want someone to volunteer to help Mark bring a new bed from 'F' dorm and take his old bed to the tip in the yard." The dorm was silent. "Well Mark, it looks like you will have to do it on your own, everyone seems to be busy."

Terry walked down the dorm towards Mark and stood in front of him. "One thing, you fucking baboon, it will only be half as heavy dumping your old bed," he continued down the dorm with three cups in his hand to make a brew.

John and Terry were sitting around the dorm table as Mark came into the dorm pushing a new bed he had collected from 'F' dorm. He was a nice shade of red and sweating like a pig. He put the bed in the centre of the dorm and went to the two halves of his old bed to remove them to the tip. He just looked at the two men drinking their tea as the two men looked back with a huge smile on their faces. It took about an hour before Mark had finished his task and he was back in the dorm making his new bed up, still very red and not looking very happy. Mark lay on his bed when it was completed, just staring into space, then a smile came over his face, he stood on his new bed and swung up onto the beam above. He sat there for a moment or two smiling down at the two men sitting at the table who were looking up at him. "Not fucking stopped me, have you? You bastards."

Terry with a knowing smile looked at John and said, "Watch this space."

The monkey on the beam, still smiling braced himself on his perch to swing to the next beam towards John and Terry. He reached out and launched himself to the next beam, as he grabbed hold his fingers slid off. It was quite a bang as he hit the

floor; the only other noise was the loud crack as he landed on his left shoulder.

"Oh dear, missed," Terry said again with a smile.

"First time I have seen him not get hold," John said.

"Yeh, first time he hadn't had grease on the beam," Terry replied.

"Grease, what fucking grease?" John replied.

Terry looked at him and said, "You know when I got the saw from the workshop, I was walking out and I saw this big tin of axle grease on the floor."

"Stop," John interrupted him. "I get the picture, but how come he was OK on the beam above his bed?"

"Simple," Terry replied, "if that one was greased he would have just fallen on his bed, however the two beams either side would have a more dramatic fall, don't you think?"

"You bastard," John said with a smile.

"Yeh aren't I just?" Terry said.

It was about two hours before Mark arrived back at the dorm with his left arm in a sling. John, Garry and Terry were sitting around John's bed after cleaning all the grease off the beams. Mark walked over to them in obvious pain. "One of you bastards are responsible for me having a broken shoulder," he said.

"Will you be able to swing with one arm?" Terry said with a smile.

"Fuck off," he replied as he walked away.

After the evening meal John was doing another drawing having gone back to the education department to collect further supplies of paper and felt pens, when a man appeared at the bottom of his bed. "You John?" the man said.

"Yes," he replied.

"You did a birthday card for one of the guys."

"Yes," John replied.

"Could you do some for the guys in our dorm?" he asked.

"Well yes, if the price is right." With that the man pulled a piece of paper out of his pocket, he unfolded it and handed it to John.

He looked at it and noticed there was a list of about six names with things like anniversary and birthdays with the name of women at the side. "When are all these needed for?" he asked the man, who was now sitting on a chair by his bed.

"Any chance of this coming Saturday?"

"Yeh, don't see why not, it's a quarter of smoke for each one, OK?"

"That's alright," the man replied as he got up off the chair.

"See you Saturday." John thought this is going crazy, I'm going to have to get even more from education. He also thought of the amount of tobacco he could accumulate if it continued.

Once more the gang of three sat round John's bed. It was eleven at night and the subject of gambling came up. "Used to love to go to the casino," Garry said.

John thought for a while, and said, "Why not have a game in here?"

Terry looked at him and said, "Point one, we don't have any cards, point two, if we get caught gambling it's a charge and point three, to even have any cards it's a charge."

John looked at them both and said, "Point one, I can get card from education and make some, point two and three, since WHEN have we been fucking concerned about breaking the rules?"

Terry and Garry looked at each other then back to John, Garry smiled and then said, "OK Mr Waddington games, make us some cards."

After work the following day John was back in the dorm armed with a supply of A3 card and some fine felt tip markers, and started to cut the card into fifty-two equal size pieces. He was about half way through the suit of spades when he noticed a new guy had taken the bed just down from him. He appeared to be somewhat upset and was lying on his bed. John stopped what he was doing and went over to the man. As he got to his bed he noticed the man had been crying.

"Hi," John said, the man looked up at him and returned the greeting. "Just arrived?"

"Yes," the man replied, looking down as a daschund's bollocks."

"Look a bit pissed off," John said to him, noticing he was only about nineteen years of age.

"Yeh, don't know what to do in here."

"Take it this is your first time then?"

"Yeh," he responded.

"Fancy a brew?" John said feeling sorry for this new guy.

"Yeh, love one, but are we allowed to?" he replied.

"No problem, any time, only thing is the waiter is off sick today," John said with a smile. John returned a few minutes later with two cups of tea. He sat down on a chair at the side of the new man's bed and handed him one of the cups. "My name's John," he said again with a smile at the man.

"I'm Brad," the man responded.

"Got a problem?" he asked the new man. "That is more than the rest of us banged up in here."

"Yeh. It's just that I am surprised at the fact that I am in prison for something I thought was no big deal."

"That goes for all of us in here," John replied. "Want to tell me?" John said.

"Yeh, I only got married two weeks ago, and a couple of days later I was in a pub when a couple of guys came in and asked if I was interested in some cheap brandy. I of course said I was, so I went outside to the car park to a car. They opened the boot of the car, and inside were two boxes of brandy. I asked them how much for three bottles, they said fifteen quid. Now I know my brandy and looking at one of the bottles knew it retailed at twenty pounds a bottle, so I said, sure make that four. They handed the bottles to me and I gave them two ten pound notes. It was then that a car that had been parked at the other side of the car park sped towards us and two guys got out one of them flashing a warrant card. The next thing I know I was in a police car and arrested for receiving stolen goods. To cut a long story short I got an eighteen month sentence."

"Eighteen months? Fuck me, that's a bit harsh for a first offence," John said thinking about Garry's eighteen months for four point five million.

"Yeh," the man replied.

"Who was your solicitor? Noddy or Big Ears?" John asked. Brad smiled, feeling a little better having someone to talk to. "Come on," John said. "Let's show you round the place, you may feel better when you see how cushy it is."

John was sitting at the large table after he returned after his guided tour with the new man. Garry came over to him and sat down. "Heard about the guy from 'E' dorm?"

"No," John replied. "What about him?"

"Let out this morning and got a gate arrest."

"Fuck me not again," he said. "Do me a favour, if you hear of any more gate arrests don't tell me. It does my head in. The cards will be finished by tonight, fancy a game after the night screw has done his inspection?"

"Yeh, I'll tell Terry and see if any of the other guys want to join us."

It was eleven o'clock and four of them were sitting around the bed with the homemade cards in a pile on top. "Well what are we playing and what are the stakes?" Terry said.

"Three card brag," replied Garry.

"OK and minimum of one roll-up and maximum of five at a time," John replied.

They all agreed as John started to deal the cards out. They had been playing for about an hour when suddenly the fire door swung open and framed in the doorway was the evening screw. They all looked at each other in shock as the screw looked at the bed to see the cards and a pile of cigarettes.

"Good evening gents," the screw said as he walked towards them. "Having a good game?" Nobody spoke, the screw picked up the cards, and said, "Right boys, I am going to tell you a little about myself. Now I close my eyes to a lot of things. You think that I walk around half blind and don't know what goes on, don't you? But I can tell you, I am not half blind and I do know what goes on, I know all about the dope, the booze and the little walkies you go on after night inspection, but I allow that to go on, because the dope makes you happy little bunnies, and happy bunnies don't get morbid and cause trouble. The booze also makes you happy and sends you to sleep. This makes life easy for me as I don't have trouble during my night shift, but these," holding up the cards, "make happy bunnies into bad bunnies and causes trouble and fights which upsets my peaceful shift. You all know the penalty for having cards and gambling, but there again if I report you I have to write out a lengthy report which means I will miss my TV programmes in the office tonight, and I don't want to miss watching them. So at the risk of appearing soft I am confiscating these." Holding the cards up once more. "With the promise that if you are caught with any more, I WILL put you on report, understand?"

They all said, "Yes sir."

The screw started to walk down the dorm, but after a few steps turned round, looked at John and said, "Made a bloody good job of those cards Davidson, but stick to birthday cards in future."

They all looked at each other. "Fuck me," John said. "It was a bloody good job that was a decent screw otherwise we all would be in deep shit."

Decent screw → character? Let things pass

Handwritten note at top: BBC Documentary - Norma, bus teacher roped John in. Just after the old bus teacher left with their bus plans for cycle shop

Chapter 14

It was Friday morning and John and Garry were walking over to the education block. John was wondering what was going to happen at the filming today. Garry went into the normal education office and John made his way to the large hall where the filming of the documentary was going to take place. As he entered he noticed the room had been arranged in the shape of a horseshoe with tables and chairs. There was a great deal of activity in the room with cameras, microphones and lighting.

Norma was stood talking to one of the men. As she noticed John walk in, she motioned for him to join them. "This is David Grayson," she said to him. "David this is John." John shook the man's hand.

"Hi," the man said, "I'm the director." He pointed round the room and said, "I want you to sit at the top of that table over there and direct the questions to the men that will be sitting around the tables each side. Norma will be sat at the side of you." When he had finished his instruction he wished John all the best and walked over to one of the men with a camera.

John and Norma walked over to their seats and sat down as Norma handed him a sheet of paper with various questions on, all based on prison reform and how the inmates felt about changes in the system. John looked down the sheet and came to one about non-violent criminals who would not be locked up full time but only at weekends and holiday times. He looked at Norma and said, "I think that question is a bit stupid. Everyone is going to agree to that?"

"We will see," she replied.

A few minutes later the men, about twenty in all started to come into the room and took their seats. When they were all settled, David Grayson stood at the back of him and Norma and addressed the men. "Good morning gentlemen, I'm David and I am the director for this short film, John," he said pointing to him, "will be asking the questions and throwing various ideas to you. If you wish to reply, may I ask you to raise your hands. Could I also ask you to watch your language to avoid us having to put too many bleeps in." Most of the men smiled.

"Right let's start," the director said, and with that another man stood in the centre of the tables and looked into a camera lens. He started to say what it was all about – things like being held in one of Her Majesty's prisons and all the men were serving a prison sentence for one thing or another and the question master was also serving a custodial sentence. After a couple of minutes he said, "I will now hand you over to our question master."

John's first question was the men's feelings on an open prison against a lock up. This prompted quite a mixed response to John's surprise. Most of the men agreed it was far better. However two of the men found it hard due to the temptation of being able to just stride over a wall – in particular at times of stress if something happened with the family like a death, or finding out that the wife was having it away with someone while they were banged up and the temptation to go to the funeral or to go and kick fuck out of the guy your wife was messing about with. All the questions and suggestions were met by a good response even though the language was not quite as choice as the director would have liked.

At last John came to the idea of part-time lock up, and explained to the men. "Right, the next one is a system which has been tried in a few countries and we would like to know your feelings on it in this country? What it would mean, would be for non-violent crimes you would be able to stay on the outside to continue with your family life, keep your jobs and therefore support your family, not having to be away from your children, but you would serve the duration of your sentence at weekends, bank holidays and your normal work's holidays. What do you think?"

The room erupted, and all hands went up. John pointed to one of the men. "NO fucking way," the man said. "It would mean I would be in and out of nick for the next five years."

"YEH," all the other men responded. John was surprised at the response. "I think the best way is to have a show of hands, all those who would NOT like that system to be introduced please put your hands up." Every hand went up. John could not believe it, it was exactly the opposite of what he had expected. He just looked at Norma who looked back with a smile on her face and mouthed, told you so. The rest of the questions were met by the same enthusiastic response from the men, and then it was over with the man who opened the forum thanking every one and the director saying cut.

David Grayson came over to them with a smile on his face. "Great," he said. "That was very good, I was surprised how well all the men joined in," and shook John's hand.

Back at the dorm that night John was telling Garry all about the filming and the response from the men, in particular the question of part-time lock up. To his surprise Garry agreed with the men.

It was about eight thirty and Garry, Terry and John were sitting round John's bed having a smoke and drinking tea when they noticed a bit of a commotion on the corridor with screws running up and down. "What the fuck's going on?" Garry said.

Terry just shrugged his shoulders as he got up to walk to the bottom of the dorm. As he got to the corridor he was met by one of the screws who stopped him and said, "Back inside."

"It's only eight thirty," Terry said, as he noticed all the other guys were being sent back to their dorms.

"Inside," the screw repeated, giving Terry a little push to help him. He did as he was told and returned to John's bed.

"What's going on?" Garry asked.

"Don't know," Terry replied, "but must be something heavy. All the guys are being sent back to their dorms."

As they looked down the dorm they saw the new guy with the one leg limping into the dorm. Eventually he came over to the three of them and said, "Have you heard yet?"

"Heard what?" John said as he got off his chair to let the man sit down.

"Well I was sat in the TV room watching a film and that swinging monkey with the sling on was sat across the way from me. Suddenly he shouted and fell on the floor – it seems one of the guys sat behind him stuck a screwdriver in his back."

"Fuck me," Terry said.

"Is he bad?" asked John.

"Don't know but the screws are going ape shit."

"Well, looks like our Mark has pissed someone off real bad," Garry put in.

About an hour later Barry the blue band came out of his room and into the dorm. He stood at the bottom and said, "Listen guys, no parade tomorrow morning and no leaving the dorm until you are instructed, OK?"

Saturday morning came and all the guys in the dorm were in small groups talking about the previous night's entertainment when a senior screw came into the dorm with a police officer by his side. "I want all men who were in the dorm between eight fifteen and eight thirty to step forward," the screw said. John, Terry and Garry stepped forward along with some of the other guys. "All you men did not leave the dorm between that time?"

"No," they all said together.

"You," he said to Garry, "come over here." He walked over to the blue band's room along with the police officer and went inside. When inside he said to Garry, "Who were you with, if anybody, during that time?" Garry told him he was sat round John's bed with Terry. "OK," the screw replied. "Go back to your bed and stand by it. Do NOT speak to anybody on the way, understand?"

"Yes sir," Garry replied and left the room with the screw. He went over to his bed as instructed to see John following the screw into the blue band's room.

A short while later John came out of the room and walked up to his bed and stood by the side of it. Garry knew that they were confirming that they had been where they were and who they were with.

After about half an hour all the men had been in the blue band's room and were standing by their beds. "Right, all those stood by your beds that we have spoken to, can leave, but nobody goes up to the TV room or games room area, understood?" the screw said.

They all left the dorm via the fire door and stood around outside talking. "What a fucking good job we didn't go and watch television last night," Terry said. "I think we would have been prime suspects after the stroke we pulled greasing the beams."

"Too bloody true," Garry replied.

At the end of the day everyone in the nick had been seen and had been allowed to go apart from twenty men who had been in the TV room the previous night and they had been taken to the room where the filming had taken place for further questions. They had found out from one of the more friendly screws that ↙ Mark the baboon was in hospital with a punctured lung.

Back at the dorm, the gang of three were sitting at the large table. John was putting the finishing touches to all the cards he had done for the other inmates just as the man who put in the order for the cards came into the dorm and came over to John. "That was good timing," John said to him, as he handed a bundle of cards over to him.

The man went through the cards and said, "These are fucking great."

"Thanks," John said. "Got the smoke?" The man reached into his pocket and pulled out six half ounce tobacco packs and handed them to John. "Cheers," he said to the man and put them in his pocket.

"Look," the man said, "one of the lads has got an anniversary next week and would like a fucking big card about eighteen inches by twelve, any chance?"

"Sure, same half ounce?"

"Yeh, no problem," as the man walked out of the dorm.

John said, "Fuck me, I've no bloody card left."

"Can't you get some more?" Terry said, thinking the more work John got the more smoke was available.

"Suppose so, I'll go over to education and raid the stores cupboard again."

"It's Saturday," Garry said.

"That's all right the door is left open," John replied. With that he got up from the table and set off out of the dorm in the direction of the education block.

He was inside education loaded up with card and coloured sheets of paper when the door opened. John looked round to see framed in the doorway the form of Mr McKay, the principle education officer. "PUT IT BACK," the man said. John put it down on one of the desks. "What are you doing in here?"

"Collecting some stationery for course work," John replied.

The man looked at John with a smirk on his face. "And who said you could help yourself?" the man said. Now the smirk had gone and was replaced with a frown.

"Grant the education teacher," John replied.

"Oh, Grant, it may have come to your notice that he left us some time ago."

John felt his stomach knot. "Yes, but I still need material for the course," John replied, now with a feeling of panic coming over him.

"And just what are you undertaking at the moment that requires that?" pointing to the pile of paper on the desk in front of John.

He had to think fast, he realised he was in deep shit. "Well it's a separate project I was working on, and wanted to work on it over the weekend to present to Norma on Monday," he replied.

"Very good," Mr McKay replied again with that sarcastic smile on his face. "Perhaps you would like to present it to the governor and myself on Monday. Shall we say nine o'clock prompt, in my office?" with that the nasty bastard started to walk back out of the room. As he did so he turned round and looked at John. "Oh, by the way put all that back," pointing to the card and papers on the desk.

John walked back to the dorm and over to the table where Terry and Garry were still sitting with a cup of tea in front of them. They looked up at him and Garry said, "What the fuck's up with you?" he had noticed by John's face that something was wrong.

John started to tell them about his brush with McKay and the summons to his office in front of the governor on Monday. When he had finished they were silent for a while and just looked at him.

"Fuck me," Terry said. "That sounds bad."

"Tell me about it," John said.

Monday at eight forty-five, John was sat on a chair outside Mr McKay's office dreading what was going to happen to him. He had a bad night with dreams of gate arrest, loss of remission and not seeing Amy and the children for even longer. The door of the office was opened by one of the screws who told him to come inside. John entered with the screw by his side. Sitting behind a large desk was the governor looking at some papers and McKay standing at the side of the desk.

The governor looked up from the papers he was reading and looked at John. "Well Davidson, what's this I have been hearing from Mr McKay?"

By now John had decide to come clean, not because he felt guilty, but because he could not think of anything plausible to say to talk his way out of the situation. "I was using the materials for my hobby of art sir," he replied.

The governor looked up at him with a frown. "I think I remember you, aren't you the man with the pictures on the wall round his bed?"

"Yes sir," John replied.

"From what I remember they were very good," the governor said. "It's only a pity you did not obtain the materials you required from the art class instead of the education store room."

"I wasn't aware I could do that sir," he lied.

out of education

"Well Davidson, Mr McKay has informed me that he no longer wishes you to be in the education department as from today, so what are we to do with you?" With that he looked back down at the papers on his desk. After a few seconds he looked back up at John and said, "Under the circumstances, I suggest you report to Mr Rains in ground maintenance, the officer will take you over to him when you leave the office. I want you to know that I decided not to take any further action due to the fact that this is the first time you have put your foot over the line, so to speak, but rest assured if you breach any further rules I will not be so lenient, now go with the officer."

"Yes sir and thank you," John replied and at the same time looking at McKay. His face was quite a cute shade of purple with temper, at him not being put on a charge.

John and the officer walked across the yard towards the maintenance hut, a few flakes of snow had started come down. Sod's law, John thought, first day working outside and it's started to snow. As they got to the door of the hut a screw came out to meet them. It was the nasty bastard who had seen him after the punch up with Terry.

"Well hello," he said with a smile on his face. "We meet again. I understand from the radio call I received that you have come over to my little bunch," Mr Rains said to John.

"Yes," John replied.

"SIR or Mr Rains after yes, fucking understand Davidson?"

"Yes Mr Rains," John answered, wanting to punch the arrogant bastard in the face.

"Right Frank leave him with me," he said to the screw who had taken him from the governor's office. He looked at John, and said, "OK. Let's get your kit for you." He walked over to a large cupboard. "First, get yourself some overalls, boots, gloves and waterproofs. You are going to need the waterproofs, I can assure you," he said again with a smile. "Think you could take the piss out of me with self inflicted hand injury did you? Well it's my turn now you bastard."

John collected his things, and put them on. When he had finished the screw said, "Right follow me," and walked out of the hut. John followed him across the yard and over to the garden area. The snow had started to fall quite heavy by now and he was thankful for the waterproof clothes he had on. They walked over to a group of men clearing a field of winter vegetables – one of them was Terry. "Right you will be working here today, that man over there will instruct you what to do," pointing at Terry. He obviously thought that he was putting the rat with the terrier, not knowing that they had become firm friends.

He walked over to Terry who had stopped work and was looking at him with a questioned look on his face, "What the fuck are you doing over here?" he said to John.

"Got kicked out of education," he replied. "What are we doing?" John asked Terry.

"Well we have got to clear this field of all the old vegetables and put them in that trailer over there," he said pointing to a large wooden trailer which was about one hundred yards away.

"Why not bring the trailer closer to where we are working?" John asked.

"Because that is too easy," Terry replied. "Why make it easy when with a little effort you can make thing as difficult as fuck? That's the way Rains thinks."

The work was hard and in spite of the gloves, John's hands were freezing. Lunchtime came and they walked over to the canteen. "Make it quick," Terry said. "I've got something in the greenhouse to warm us up before we start back." They finished their meal and started back across the yard towards the greenhouse. As they entered John noticed that Brad, the new guy who had got eighteen months for receiving the brandy, was sitting on a box in the corner of the greenhouse.

"Hi," John said. "Didn't know you were on maintenance."

"Yeh," the man replied, "gave me this I think just to piss me off even more."

Terry looked at John and said in a whisper, "I don't know this guy too well, is he OK?"

"Sure," John replied and introduced them both. With that Terry walked over to a pile of plant pots at the side of the greenhouse and started to remove them one by one. Finally he got to one near the bottom and removed a bottle.

"Fancy a whiskey?" he asked John.

"Whiskey? Sure do," John replied. Terry took a drink out of the bottle and then handed it to John who in turn took a drink. He looked at Terry and nodded to Brad who had been watching in anticipation. Terry nodded his approval, John handed the bottle to Brad who took it with a note of thanks, and in turn took a drink and the passed it back to Terry. By now it was time to return to the field and the clearing of the field and the long trek backwards and forwards to the trailer.

At last it was time to finish for the day. By now the snow had come down quite heavy and the ground was covered by snow to the depth of about two inches. "Going to be deep tomorrow," Terry said, as they walked back to the hut to put their tools away.

Back at the dorm John was happy to have a warm shower and thank God he had got through his first day, a bit different to the cushy education department he thought.

The next morning John awoke to find the snow had continued most of the night to cover the ground to a depth of about four or five inches. The gang of three had breakfast and Garry went off to his nice warm education department and John and Terry went off to the maintenance hut to change into their work clothes, Rains the screw was waiting for them. "Good morning gentlemen," he said with his normal sarcasm. "Ready for work on this lovely day?" John just looked at him with a smile to match his sarcasm. "Davidson," the screw said. "I have a special job for you today."

"Yes sir, and what would that be?"

The screw smiled even broader. "Litter clearance," he replied.

"Litter clearance?"

"Yep, litter clearance, in the yard and the car park, I want you to collect all the litter and put it into a black bag," he said pointing to a pile of dustbin liners in the corner of the room.

"Could I just make a point sir?" John replied.

"What?" the screw responded.

John looked at him, and said, "The point is sir, we have about four inches of snow on the ground and all the litter is underneath it."

"Oh yes, that's another point, you may as well clear the snow to find the litter while you are about it." John just looked at him. He knew now that this bastard was going to give him all the worst and stupid jobs that came up.

John was in the car park clearing the snow and looking for litter when one of the screws from the gatehouse came over to him. "What the fuck are you doing?" he asked him.

"Collecting litter," John replied.

"Collecting litter?" the screw said. "Who in God's name gave you that job?"

"Mr Rains," John replied.

"WHAT a surprise," the man said with a bit of a scowl on his face. "Come with me." With that started walking back to the gatehouse, John followed and went into the gatehouse where there was another screw.

"Want a brew?" the first screw asked John.

"Wouldn't mind," John replied. And with that the screw went over to a small boiler and made John a cup of tea. As he sat down on a chair to have his drink the first screw was relating the story to his fellow officer who was shaking his head as the story unfolded. He finished his tea and thanked the two officers, who said, "OK carry on, there is nothing we can do but this is bang out of order what you are expected to do."

John was just walking out of the gatehouse when he noticed two men in prison dress sitting on the wall with their legs over the wall. "Excuse me," John said to the two screws, "but two guys are sat on the wall."

"Yes," one of the screws said, "been there for about two hours."

"But they are the wrong side of the nick," John said.

"Yes they have sent a message to the governor that they want to go back to a closed nick, and the boss has refused, so they in effect have absconded which means a charge and automatically means a return to a closed nick, but we will leave them out there for another couple of hours to cool of so to speak, and then go and get them. We should charge them, but we will give them the opportunity of deciding to stay here or being charged and shipped out." John was surprised he had found a screw that appeared to be human.

The rest of the day he continued with his task of finding bits of paper under the snow with his welcome break for lunch which he had with Garry. "How's it going?" Garry asked.

"How's it going? I'm fucking freezing, wet, and pissed off, that's how it's going," John replied. "Mark my words, I am going to get back at that bastard Rains. I don't know how but I will find some way."

John was glad to be back at the dorm after his day of torture. He was sitting at the table with Garry, Terry and Brad having a cup of tea. "That bastard Rains sure has it in for you," Terry said.

"Yeh," he replied, "but I can bide my time, there must be some way I can get back at him."

"One of the lads at the bottom of the dorm goes out tomorrow," Garry said.

"So it looks like we have a bed to string up tonight."

"Don't think so," Terry put in. "The screws have put a stop to it since one fell down and landed on top of one of the guys in 'F' dorm and damn near killed the poor bastard."

"There must be something we can give him as a parting present," Garry said. They fell silent for a short while trying to think of something they could do.

Suddenly Terry said, "Is the print room working late tonight?"

"Yeh they finish at six thirty," John replied. With that Terry got up and went down the dorm and out to the print shop. He returned about half an hour later with a small tin. He came over to them and sat down.

"What have you got there?" Brad asked.

"Blue ink," Terry replied.

"What the fuck have you got that for?" John asked.

"Well you know most of the guys have a shower on their last night, well I thought it would be a bit of fun to throw a tin of ink over him so he could go out in a blaze of colour so to speak."

John smiled, "Yeh but what you haven't thought of, if he's in the shower it will wash straight off him."

Garry said, "Yeh, but some should stick."

They were all sitting around John's bed sharing a joint and all eyes were focused on the man down the dorm, willing him to go and have a shower. It was about eight thirty and the man went to his locker and took out his towel and walked towards the shower room.

"Right give him five minutes," Terry said.

Five minutes went by and the four of them got up and went down the dorm to the shower room. As they entered they could hear the shower running in one of the shower cubicles. Terry had taken the top off the can of ink. Garry had hold of the cubicle door handle and nodded to Terry, "NOW," he shouted to Terry, as he pulled the door open.

Terry threw the ink over the man as his back was turned. Garry quickly closed the door and they all ran back into the dorm and sat back at John's bed. About two minutes later the man came out of the shower room and walked back to his locker and put his towel back in; the four of them looked at each other.

"It's not worked," John said. "I told you it would wash off him."

The next minute another man came out of the shower room vivid blue, they all looked at each other with their mouths open.

"Fuck me," Terry said, wrong cubicle. The man screamed up the dorm.

"OK, which bastard did this?" Nobody owned up as the man went back into the shower room to wash the ink off. He came out about half an hour later still blue. They and the rest of the dorm found it hard to suppress a laugh. As he went back to his bed John reached under his bed for the empty can of ink. "Did you look at the label on the can?" he asked Terry.

"Yes," he replied.

"And what did it say?" John again asked.

"Blue ink," Terry replied.

"Did you happen to read the reverse side on the tin?"

"No," Terry said.

"Then I will read it to you." John started to read the back of the tin. "This is an oil based dye and indelible. If it come into contact with the skin it could take up to three weeks before the colour vanishes." They all looked at Terry who by now was curled up in a fit of laughter.

"I wouldn't laugh too much," Garry said with a smile, "if that bloke finds out it was you who got the ink he is going to rip your fucking head off." By now they were all laughing about the blue man.

The night screw came in the dorm to do his evening inspection; as usual he walked up the dorm looking at each of the men. As he got to the bed of the blue man who was lying on the top with just a pair of trousers on, he stopped, took a long look and said, "Oh yes, very pretty," Then continued up the dorm without any further comment until he arrived at John's bed with the four of them round it. He looked at the four and with a smile on his face said, "I am not even going to ask if you had anything to do with that," as he pointed his thumb over his shoulder at the blue man.

Chapter 15

The following morning they were once more in the canteen having breakfast when the blue man came through the door. All the men in the canteen burst into laughter as he walked in. John looked up and noticed that some of the dye had caught him on one side of his head. As he walked past the first table, one of the guys turned and said with a laugh, "What a fucking awful birth mark."

"Fuck off," the man replied.

It was as they were leaving the canteen they noticed a screw on a bike riding past. John noticed it was Rains. He rode past them, got off his bike and leaned it against the medical section wall facing the canteen. He took a chain that was around his neck and secured it with a padlock to the drain pipe and the front wheel.

"Hope he falls off and breaks his fucking neck," John said to Terry.

"No such luck," Terry replied.

Garry left them and set off in the direction of the education department as they continued on their journey to the maintenance hut. As they got there Rains was waiting for them. He instructed Terry and some of the other men to continue with the work they were doing the previous day, and with that sarcastic smile turned to John and said, "Well, the snow has melted a bit today so it will make it a bit easier to find your litter today."

"Oh goody," John replied with a smile on his face to match the sarcastic one on the screw's face.

"Don't get funny with with me Davidson, now get on your way," he said.

The next few days went by without much change. John continued with his litter duties and the nights were made up of talking and having a joint around his bed. At last it was Friday night and the now gang of four were sitting around the table drinking tea when the man from the other dorm who had asked for all the cards to be done came in and walked over to the table.

"Can you do tattoos?" he asked John.

John looked up at him, "Tattoos? Well I don't see why not, that is if I had a tattoo gun."

"Got one, a guy in our dorm made a battery one out of an old staple gun and we have got the ink from the print room."

"Hang on," Garry said, "that's a serious charge offence."

"It's worth a good drink," the man from the other dorm said.

John thought for a moment and then said, "Full bottle of scotch upfront."

"Fuck me," the man said. "That's a bit heavy."

"So is the charge if I get caught," John replied.

"I'll let you know," the man said and walked out of the dorm. Half an hour later he was back and told John his man had agreed to the scotch.

"What does he want?" John asked.

"An eagle," the man replied.

"That's OK," John said. "Tell him to come on Sunday about seven, oh and the scotch tomorrow."

"OK," the man said, "I'll bring the whiskey in the morning."

"No," John replied, "don't bring it in the dorm, put it behind the plant pots in the greenhouse."

"OK," he said, as he left the dorm.

He turned to the three men with him and with a big smile said, "Party time tomorrow in the greenhouse."

Terry rubbed his hands and said, "I'll bring a block of blow I was saving."

The four of them left the canteen after lunch and walked over to the greenhouse. They went inside and John went to the pile of plant pots in the corner. A few seconds later he was holding a bottle of Grouse whiskey. "Drinky time," he said to his comrades.

They all sat down on some old boxes and John opened the bottle as Terry was rolling a joint. John passed the bottle round and Terry passed the joint. When it came to Brad he refused the joint saying he did not smoke dope, but after a bit of persuasion from Terry, took it out of his hand and took a long drag. After about half an hour the bottle was almost empty and they had smoked about six joints, Brad was looking a little the worst for wear and Garry asked him if he was OK.

"Fine," he replied with somewhat of a slur in his speech. They finished the scotch and John noticed Brad was falling to sleep.

"Come on. Let's get back," John said. They all stood up to walk out, that was when Brad fell over. He lay on the floor as they all went to help him, but try as they may they could not rouse him from his drunken stupor.

"We can't take him back to the dorm like this," Garry said.

"Well we can't leave him here," John said.

Terry looked outside the greenhouse, "I know," he said. Let's throw him in the compost heap and come back for him later."

"We can't throw him in the fucking compost heap, what happens if someone walks past and sees him?" John said.

"We can cover him up with some of the compost," Terry replied.

They all agreed that was the only option left open to them. They all carried him outside and put him at the back of the heap of compost. Terry collected a load of rhubarb leaves and covered him up.

"This is all your fault," John said to Terry.

"MY fault how do you work that out?"

"You gave him the fucking joint."

"Yes, and YOU gave him the fucking whiskey."

"Come on," Garry said. "We will have to collect him later." They all went back to the dorm to have a lie down.

They all fell asleep and when they awoke congregated around John's bed drinking tea and having a cigarette. Garry looked up at the clock on the wall. "Fuck me. I forgot about Brad, it's three hours since we left him."

The words were hardly out of his mouth when a garbage-covered figure was seen walking up the dorm towards them. All the guys in the dorm stopped what they were doing and stared at the bedraggled man; the three round the bed just burst into laughter.

"What does he look like?" Terry said, as he reached the bed.

"What the fuck happened?" Brad asked brushing what was left of a carrot off the top of his head.

"You got pissed," replied John.

"Yeh, but did you have to throw me in the fucking rubbish dump?"

"Yes," they all said at the same time.

"Look," John said, "there was no way we could bring you back to the dorm, and we had to hide you somewhere until you sobered up."

"Yeh, that's fair enough, but the rubbish dump?"

"Look why not go and get a shower and I will make you a brew," John said.

"Yeh OK," Brad replied as he walked to his locker to get his towel and some clean clothes.

The rest of Saturday went without any further event. The four of them sat around the dorm apart from an hour in the evening when they went to the TV room to watch part of a film, which half way through, turned out to be lousy so they all went back to the dorm where John started to draw various eagles in anticipation of his tattoo customer the following night. About eleven o'clock the effect of their little party was taking its toll and they all decided to call it a day and turn in for the night.

The following evening they were once more sitting round the table when the man from the other dorm came into the dorm with a man John had not seen before. They both walked over to the table and the man introduced the new man as Sean.

"Hi," John said, assuming this was the guy he was to give the tattoo.

The man responded by saying, "Have you got any pictures I can look at?"

"You mean pictures of eagles?" John said.

"Yeh," the man replied. John went over to his locker and collected six pictures he had produced and brought them over to the man and put them down in front of him. Sean picked up the drawings and started looking at them one by one. As he came to the last one he turned and looked at John and said, "These are fucking great."

John asked, "Which one would you like?"

"All of them," the man replied with a smile, "but can't find enough whiskey for you."

"Right," John said, "what's the situation with the ink and the needle gun?" With that the man put his hand in his pocket and produced three bottles of ink, red, blue and black. He then pulled a converted stapler out and put it on the table.

John picked it up and looked at it. It had twin needles each at the side of each other. "How does it work?" John asked. Sean took it out of his hand and connected two wires that led to a small battery. As he connected the wires the contraption jumped into life like a small sewing machine. He smiled and looked at John.

"Well what do you think?" he asked.

"Amazing," John replied.

Sean was sitting on a chair at the side of John's bed. Brad was sitting on another chair and Terry was at the bottom of the dorm keeping watch along the corridor. John sat facing the man with a fine black felt pen in his hand. He started to draw the outline of an eagle in full flight on Sean's right shoulder. "Right," John said, "let's get on with it." As he opened the first bottle of ink, he got the battery powered gismo and connected the two wires; the make shift tattoo gun whirled into action. He applied some of the black ink to a piece of cotton wool and rubbed it around the drawing of the eagle. John applied the gun to Sean's shoulder and carefully followed the line of the eagle.

He stopped and wiped the blood away and the excess ink, to John's surprise and relief he saw a perfect black line that followed the contour of the eagle's wing for about one inch.

Just over an hour later John wiped the last of the ink and blood off Sean's shoulder and stood up to admire his handiwork. "Perfect," he said with pride. "Absolutely fucking perfect."

Brad went round the back of Sean to look at the finished tattoo. "Fucking hell," he said. "You have even got the veins in the feathers."

"Yeh, ain't I just," John replied with a huge smile. Sean got up off the chair and thanked John. "Make sure you keep your shirt on for the next week in case any screws are about. It will take that long for it to scab over and if any of the screws see it before that they will know it is a new tattoo and start asking questions. Remember it is just as much a charge for you to have one done in here as it is for me to do one." Sean once more thanked John and set off back down the dorm.

They were all once more sat round John's bed, with Brad going on about how fantastic the tattoo was, suddenly he turned to John and said, "I want one."

"YOU want one?" John said.

"Yeh, want one with my wife's name," he replied.

"What's your wife's name?" John asked.

"Tina," Brad answered.

"So you just want the name?"

"Well no," he said looking a bit embarrassed.

"Well what do you want?"

"Well I thought I would have, Brad heart Tina, you know. Brad then a heart and then Tina underneath."

"Yeh get the picture," John said with a smile. By now Terry was rolling around on the floor in fits of laughter.

"I don't think that's funny, in fact I think it is quite romantic," Garry said, just before he fell about laughing.

"Fuck off," Brad responded.

"OK give me until tomorrow and I'll do some drawings for you to look at."

Monday morning came around again and John and his two co-workers were walking across the yard to the work hut. When they arrived the first thing they noticed was that McKay was not waiting for them.

"Where is the bastard?" Terry said.

"Maybe he has fallen off his bike and broken his fucking neck," John replied.

"No such luck," Brad said, as they were waiting for him to arrive.

John was looking round the work hut at all the tools in rows on the walls: hammers, pliers, spanners. John stopped and looked at Terry and Brad, "What did you say before Brad?"

"What?"

"About 'no such luck'?"

"Yeh, no such luck he would fall off his bike." John went over to the tools on the wall and took a set of spanners off the wall. He looked round at the two of them with a smile. "Why not make our own luck?" he said to the two of them.

"What do you mean, make our own luck?" Terry said with a worried look on his face.

"Put it this way," John replied with an even broader smile, "do you think one of these spanners would fit the wheel nuts on a bike?"

"Oh, no," Terry replied. "I hope you are not thinking what I think you are thinking?" He stopped and then said, "You are aren't you?" John just smiled.

"NO FUCKING WAY," Brad responded. John ignored them both and put two of the spanners in his pocket and returned the remainder back on the wall just as Rains walked in.

They were sitting down in the canteen at lunchtime when John got up from the table saying he was just going outside for a moment. Ten minutes later he returned with a beaming smile all over his face. Terry and Brad looked at each other and then back at John. "Tell me you haven't," Terry said with a look of dread on his face.

"Oh yes I have," John replied.

"You have removed the wheels from his bike?"

"Nope, just the front one, well NOT exactly removed it, more undid it."

"How much?" Terry asked.

"Well I did remove it, then put it back on half a turn."

"I suppose you do realise that if, or rather when, the wheel falls off he is going to go straight over the fucking handle bars."

"Yep," John replied with a grin.

They finished work for the day and set off back to the dorm, when John said, "Before we go back, fancy a bit of a walk?"

"A walk, where to?" asked Terry?

"Oh, I just thought we could have a walk round the canteen and past the medical block."

Terry and Brad looked at each other. "Don't you think we, or should I say you, should stay as far away as possible from that area?" Brad replied.

"Not a chance," John said with a smile. "Wouldn't miss this for the fucking world."

They got to the canteen just in time to see McKay bending down and putting on his cycle clips. He undid the chain from the bikes wheel and put it around his neck. Cocking his leg over the frame of the bike he set off towards the gatehouse to leave the nick to go home. He had gone about one hundred yards and everything was going fine.

"Fuck it," John said. "I must have put the nuts on too well."

It was just after that as the bike and its rider were going down a slight incline round a bend, the bike suddenly went nose down and stopped. However, the front wheel continued on its journey followed by it's rider. McKay flew for about six feet over the handlebars before coming to a crumpled heap on the floor.

"BINGO!" John half shouted. "Time for a cup of tea," he said with a satisfied look on his face.

As they left the crime scene and walked back to the dorm, Terry said, "You crazy bastard, you could have caused him serious injury."

"YEP," John replied with a smile.

As they got to the dorm Garry was sitting at the table with four cups of tea in front of him that he had made in anticipation of their return from work. They thanked him and sat down. Garry looked at John who had a huge grin on his face. He looked at the two other men and nodded towards John. "What's he so happy about?" Terry started to tell him all that had gone on. "Fucking hell, did he hurt himself?"

"Fucking hope so," John replied.

"You still want that tattoo?" John asked Brad as they sat around his bed.

"Sure do," he replied.

John handed him the drawings he had done and said, "Well we had better do it tonight, the guy from the other dorm wants the equipment and the ink back tomorrow."

Brad looked at the drawings, and chose one about one and a half inches in diameter with blue writing and a red heart in the centre.

"OK, leave it till about seven thirty and I will get it done for you. Oh by the way, where do you want it?"

"On my forearm," Brad replied.

"No fucking way," John said. "It's too easy for the screws to see if your sleeves rolled up."

Brad thought for a while, and then said, "I know, on my arse."

"On your arse?" Garry said with a laugh.

"Well yes, the screws won't see it there will they?"

"Hang on a minute," John said, "you want ME to touch your arse?"

"Why not?" Brad replied. "I had a shower last night."

The other three just looked at each other and laughed.

"OK, your arse it is," John said.

Seven thirty came and Brad was lying face down on John's bed with his trousers round his knees. The others were gathered round waiting to see the look on John's face as he started to draw the outline of the tattoo. John got his felt tip and started writing the name and drawing the heart. Above the heart he wrote BRAD and under the heart he wrote JANE.

Terry gave him a tap on the shoulder. "Er, John, shall we make a cup of tea before you start?"

"Good idea," he replied, "you lay there, be back in a minute," he said as he set off down the dorm with four cups with teabags in.

Terry looked at John, "I think you have made a mistake."

"Why?" John asked.

"Well from what I understand Brad's wife's name is Tina."

"Yep," John replied with a grin.

"Well you have drawn on his arse the name Jane."

"Yeh, would you like to be a fly on the wall the first night he gets undressed when he gets out?"

"You bastard," Terry said.

They walked back to John's bed area with the cups of tea and John started work on the tattoo. After a short while, which seemed a long time to Brad, the job was finished. "How does it look?" Brad asked.

Garry who had been wised up by now to the trick John was up to, said, "Fucking great I think your wife is going to be well surprised, when she sees it. I think it will make all the difference to your sex life when you get out." Garry looked at John with a huge smile, and at the same time mouthed, you bastard, John smiled back and nodded in agreement.

The following morning they were back in the work hut after walking across the yard in pouring rain. By the time they got there they were soaking wet. Rains was not in the hut and Terry said, "The bastard's late again."

"Yeh, maybe John has killed the fucker," Brad replied. Just then a screw walked into the hut.

"Good morning," he said. John immediately noticed it was the man from the gatehouse who had given him a cup of tea when he was collecting litter from under the snow in the car park.

"Good morning officer," John replied. The other two looked at him, and thought OFFICER, what the fuck is this officer bit? The screw looked at John and said, "Ah, so we meet again."

"Yes sir," John replied, "and may I apologise, I don't think I thanked you for the cup of tea the other day." John had told the lads about the good screw who had taken him into the gatehouse and given him a warm drink, and wanted to let them know that this was the screw.

"That's OK," the screw replied. "Now my name is Gregson, and I have taken over Mr Rains' duties for the time being. Mr Rains is off sick at present, so you will report to myself as you did to him."

Terry turned to John and said, "Maybe you can do a get well card for him?"

"How about a get dead card," he replied. The guys in the hut laughed, and John thought he even saw a smile on the screw's face. Terry said, "I hope he is not too good, sorry I meant bad?"

The screw looked at him and said, "I will accept that slip of the tongue. Right I have been looking at the work sheets for the past few weeks, and notice you have been on outside duties. I don't think you should work outside today, as you will not be able to undertake the work in this rain, so, you two," pointing to John and Terry, "will clean inside the full length of the corridor windows, and the rest of you will work in the greenhouse, getting it tidy for the spring planting." John thought, this guy is giving us cushy inside jobs to keep us out of the rain. "Is that clear?" the screw said.

"Sure is Mr Gregson," most of them replied.

"OK then get on with your jobs. You two," he said, to John and Terry, "do me a favour, before you leave the hut, dry yourself off and put your waterproofs on. I don't want you dripping water all over the corridor," with that he left the hut.

They stayed about half an hour drying off and then collected all the cleaning materials from the hut, put on their waterproofs and walked back over the yard to the dorms.

John started at the bottom of the corridor and Terry walked up to the far end with the idea of meeting in the middle, when they had completed the cleaning. It was near to lunchtime when they met up having done the windows along the full length of the corridor. They had done a good job and the windows were gleaming. Mr Gregson came into where they had been working, he looked round, without comment, and then said after looking through the windows, "Still a bloody awful day."

"Yes sir," John replied.

"Have you finished?" the screw asked.

"Yes sir," Terry replied.

Gregson walked down the corridor inspecting the windows, when he returned, he turned to John, and said, "Well time to eat, and after you have it's back to working outside." John thought, fuck me what a day to get covered in mud. "However," the screw said, "I am not happy with the windows and I think you should do them over again, but this time I want you to take your time and do them properly, that should take you to finish of work today, do I make myself understood?"

"Yes sir," John replied. The screw reached in his tunic pocket and brought out a packet of Benson and Hedges King size, he took two out and threw them on the window ledge. "Right get off to lunch," he turned round and walked down the corridor.

John and Terry just looked at each other, "Is that a good screw or is that a good screw," they said as they picked up the cigarettes and walked towards the canteen.

They sat down after getting the food and were joined by Brad and Garry. "How's it going?" Brad asked.

"Fucking great," John replied, and told him all about the new screw Gregson, including the cigarettes.

"He sounds a good guy," Garry replied.

"Sure is, only hope we keep him, rather than that other bastard."

"I agree," Brad said, "all we have done is sit around and moved a few plant pots around."

They finished their lunch and John and Terry were back on the corridor. The rain was still pouring down, and they were grateful for being inside where it was warm and dry. John said, "Well what are we supposed to do with the windows, we can't possibly get them any cleaner?"

"Just go through the motions I suppose," Terry replied. So they just went from top to bottom of the corridor giving a bit of a polish here and a bit of a polish there until it was four o'clock, an hour before it was time to finish work.

When Mr Gregson came into the corridor and without looking at the windows, turned to the two of them and said, "NOW, that's a lot better, don't think it is worth starting anything new at this time, you may just as well knock off for today and go back to your dorms and have a cup of tea."

"Thanks," John replied, "and thanks for the smoke."

"Smoke, what smoke?" he said as he walked back out.

The following morning they were walking back to the work hut, the rain had stopped and the sun was beginning to come out. When they got to the hut, Mr Gregson was already waiting for them. "Good morning lads," he said. "Better day today. I think we can go back to finish the field clearance today as we have another job starting tomorrow which I think you will all like."

"What's that?" John asked.

"Well about ten minutes walk from the nick there are some stables who keep the horses and fox hounds for the local hunt, and every year they have us load all the old straw that has been cleared out of the horse stables and the dog pens for the past year onto trailers to be taken away to another farm to put on the fields."

"You mean we can take a walk on the other side of the wall without a pull?" Terry said.

"That's about it," the screw said with a smile.

"Is there a pub on the way?" John asked, the screw just looked at him and shook his head. "Too bad," John said, "been nice to pop in for a pint."

Outside they were clearing the field when one of the guys jumped back. "Fuck me," he said.

"What's the matter?" John asked.

"Fucking mice all over the place."

John and Terry walked over to the man and looked down at where the man was pointing. There under the cut down vegetables were dozens of tiny field mice. John bent down and picked one of them up. He held it in his hand for a short while and then put it back down on the ground.

"Can we keep one as a pet?" Brad asked.

"I don't think the screws would be too pleased to have mice running all over the dorm," John replied. He fell silent for a moment, "but I do know who would like them," he said. He turned to Terry, and said, "In the hut there are some boxes can you go and get one for me?" Terry ran off in the direction of the hut and came back a short while with one of the boxes in his hand. John bent down and started to collect the little mice and put them in the box. When he had collected about a dozen he closed the lid on the box and put it at the side of the field. Lunchtime came and John retrieved the box and put it under his arm.

"What the fuck are you going to do with them?" Terry asked.

"Oh I thought that bastard Mckay, the head of education may like them," he said with a smile. "You carry on to the canteen I'll join you in a minute," and with that set off to the education department and McKay's office as he knew he would have gone to lunch by now. He got back to the canteen about ten minutes later and sat down to eat his lunch, by now Terry had filled in Garry, who by now was sitting with them.

"What have you done with them?" Garry asked.

"Well I knew his office would be empty, so I took them out of the box and put them on his desk," John replied.

"Let's get this right," Garry said. "You have put twelve mice on McKay's desk?"

"Well no not all twelve. I put some in the drawers in his desk and some in the pocket of his coat that was hung up behind the door."

"You are a fucking nutcase," Terry said.

When they had finished work they went back to the dorm to find Garry sitting at the table with a smile on his face. John went over to him to find out if McKay had found his present. "Well did he find them?" he asked Garry.

"FIND them?" he replied. "He has gone fucking mental. Did you know he has a paranoid fear of mice?"

"Oh good," John replied.

"Not only that but you know the coat you put some in? Well it just so happens that it was a present from his wife she had given him only yesterday, and they have eaten one of the pockets."

John burst out laughing. "Fucking hell," he said, "there is a God after all."

Mckay nice incident possible mention when talking about John being kicked out of education

Chapter 16

After breakfast the following morning they were heading back across the yard to the work hut where they could see Mr Gregson waiting for them. "Morning guys," he said to them. "Ready for your country ramble?" They all nodded to him, thinking how nice it would be to get out of the nick and have a bit of freedom. As soon as all the other guys had arrived they started off towards the gatehouse and relative freedom from their incarceration.

They walked out of the gate and down the road towards the farm and stables where they were to spend the next few days working. John noticed that most of the property was expensive and wondered once again how they had managed to get planning permission to build an open prison in such a rural position as this, money must speak very loudly, that's all he could think.

They arrived at the stables and dog pounds within ten minutes and John noticed the house was quite an imposing place with huge gates. About fifty yards down from the main gate was a second gate leading into a yard surrounded by low buildings, some of them with horses' heads poking out of the top. At the far end of the yard there were large cages containing two dozen or so beagles all barking like hell.

They walked into the yard to be met by a tall imposing man dressed in tweeds and riding boots. "Good morning," the man said as he walked over to them. He shook Mr Gregson's hand and introduced himself. "Let me show you round the place and tell you what we want doing."

They followed the man into one of the building whose walls were covered in saddles, bridles and horse blankets. John took it to be the tack room. "Over there, you will find a kettle, tea and coffee and the milk is in the fridge, so help yourself to a drink when you want one. I would ask those of you who smoke, not to do so in here," he said with quite a pleasant smile.

They followed the man back out into the yard. He pointed to a very large pile of a mixture of straw and horse manure and a large trailer. "That is your task," he said to the screw. "All that has to be loaded onto the trailer to be removed by one of my stable hands." He pointed to another shed and said, "You will find all the tools and wheelbarrows in there," he said pointing to a large shed at the side of the tack room. "You won't see much of me as I am out most of the day. If you have any problems my wife will be in the house and she will be able to answer any questions you may have," he said to Mr Gregson.

"Fine sir," the screw replied. "I'm sure we will be fine," he replied.

"Well best of luck," the man said as he started to walk out of the yard.

"Right," Mr Gregson said, "let's get to work."

They all went over to the shed and collected pitchforks that were lined up against the wall. They went over to the pile of manure and started to load it into wheelbarrows to be taken to the trailer. Three of the men were standing by the trailer and transferred the contents of the barrows onto the trailer. Within an hour or so the trailer was about a quarter full and the screw said, "Right boys, let's have a break."

Back at the tack room one of the guys put the kettle on and the others sat around on some bales of hay. Suddenly the screw's radio started to bleep, he picked it up and answered with, "Hello, Gregson." There was silence for a short while he listened to the person on the other end. "Yes sir, no problem." He looked at John while he was talking which told John that the call involved him in some way. He switched the radio off and put it at the side of him on the bale of hay. He turned to John and said, "That was the senior officer. They want you back at the dorm straight away. I have just been asked if you could be trusted to walk back on your own and without supervision. I told them you could, so don't let me down."

"What's it about?" John asked.

"Well I think you have a spin."

"A spin what the fuck for? What are they looking for?" he asked.

The screw just looked at him with raised eyebrows. "I think you know as well as I do," he replied.

John started walking down the road back towards the nick; he had a bit of a panic wondering if he had his dope hidden enough. Just before he got to the nick he noticed a public phone box. Amy, he thought, dare I risk a quick call to her. He knew if he was seen he would be in deep shit. Fuck it, he thought, and went into the box, he picked up the phone and dialled one hundred. The operator answered. "Yes may I help you?" the voice on the other end of the phone asked.

"Yes, could you give me a transfer call?" John gave him his home number and his name. The phone rang and then he heard it picked up at the other end.

"I have a collect call for you from Cheshire, will you accept the call?" the operator asked. He heard Amy's voice say, "Yes."

"Hi doll," John said, "it's me."

John heard Amy say, "How? What? Where are you speaking from?" He could detect that she was crying at the sound of his voice. He quickly explained and told her how much he loved her, and was missing her, she replied with the same sentiment, and all too soon he had replaced the phone with somewhat of a tear in his eyes.

Amy phone conversation

When he entered the dorm he could see two screws standing by his bed. "Davidson," one of the screws said. "We want to search your belongings. We have to have you present to make sure that the search is undertaken with your permission. If you do not give your permission this other officer will remain with you while I get a compulsory search order from the governor, do you agree to the search?"

John felt a bit of a knot in his stomach as he said, "No problem, search away."

The screws emptied his locker and put everything on the bed, including all his felt pens, the fine ones and the big thick ones. When they had inspected each item including taking the bottom off each pen they put them back in his locker. The bed was taken apart, including the rubber bungs out of the legs, after half an hour they had finished and turned to him. "You are clean Davidson," and with not even a sorry walked back out of the dorm.

It was nine o'clock and the gang of four were once more sitting around John's bed. "OK," Terry said, "how the fuck did you get away with that spin. I fucking KNOW you have some."

John just smiled and said, "Fancy a bit of blow?"

"Yeh," Terry replied.

John reached into his locker and brought out a large blue felt marker and threw it over to Terry. He looked at it, and said, "Take the bottom off it."

"There's no fucking dope in this," as he handed it back to him. John took the pen from him and pulled the plastic plug out of the bottom of the pen. He then took a bit of the blue ink fibre out of the bottom; he then removed a small plug of cling film out, and then a quarter inch block of junk. "I call it a sandwich," he said to them all. "The pen works perfect and the base still has ink in it," he threw the lump of dope to Terry. "Make us a roll-up," he said with a smile.

Garry laughed, "The fucking screws had it in their hands all the time and didn't know it."

"How many pens have you got like this?" Brad asked.

"Fourteen," John replied with a grin.

The following morning they were back at the stables, clearing away the rest of the manure heap which by now was going down quite well, as they finished for another regular tea break in the tack room. John was having a walk around looking at all the saddles and the other things that were required to go and chase a little furry thing with a brush tail and then have it torn to pieces in the name of vermin control. But, of course, they did not have any otters to kill, or deer to tear to pieces in the name of culling, after all, otters did eat fish, most of which were course fish, and deer did chew on the odd tree, so why not go and destroy them with dogs who were only too pleased to rip them apart. But we must remember, John thought to himself, these hunted animals DO enjoy the chase as much as the dogs and the hunters do? BOLLOCKS, John thought to himself.

He had just turned a corner in the room when he noticed a wooden shelf on the wall. He walked over to it and picked up a bottle that stood on it. GRANTS WHISKEY it said. It was very dusty and had obviously stood on the shelf for some time, left over from one of the pre-hunt stirrup cups, John thought as he removed the top to give the contents a bit more of an inspection. He put the bottle to his nose to smell the contents. Uhm nice, he said to himself, but how would it taste? With that he decided the only way to find out was to take a sip. With a little trepidation he put the bottle to his lips and took a short drink. Bloody lovely, he again said to himself, as he replaced the top on the bottle and put it back on the shelf.

"John, tea up," he heard Terry shout from the other end of the tack room. He walked back down the room to find them all sitting on old boxes and bales of hay drinking their tea. John joined them on one of the hay bales and took a cup out of Terry's hand. Mr Gregson, the screw, was outside talking to the owner. John motioned with his head for Terry to follow him as he got up to walk back down the tack room back to his newly found booty. Terry followed him asking him what he wanted. John reached up to the shelf and took the bottle down. He looked at Terry with a broad smile. "Pass me your tea," he said to Terry. As he did as he was told as John removed the top from the bottle, John poured some into Terry's cup and then his own. "What the fuck have you put in there?"

John said, "Just drink," again Terry did as he was instructed and took a drink from the cup. "Fuck me, now that is a good brew," he said with a smile, "how the hell did you find that?"

"Just call me an alcohol bloodhound," John replied with a smile.

Mr Gregson came back into the tack room after the conversation outside with the owner and sat down on one of the bales of hay. "Well guys, it looks like tomorrow is going to be our last day, but I can tell you that the man I have just been having a talk to outside is very pleased with the work you have done and the speed you have all undertaken it. He also asked me if he could give you a bit of a reward when you have finished tomorrow." They all looked at the screw who said nothing.

"Well," John said. "What is it?"

The screw said, "Well, he wanted to know if he could leave you a small case of beer in the tack room as a thank you. I unfortunately had to tell him that you are on prison duties and it was against the rules." They all looked at him in silence.

Terry suddenly spoke up, "Look boss," he said, "we have worked fucking hard on this job and finished it in good time, and..."

The screw cut him short, "Sit down and shut up." Terry did as he was told with a frown on his face. The screw smiled and said, "I also told him that when we have finished, I would have a cup of tea with him and his wife in his house and that would take about half an hour, so I could not see what you guys were doing in the tack room," he stood up and winked. "Come on boys, let's take you home."

They were all sitting on the boxes and bales of hay the following day. They had completed the work they had to do and Mr Gregson had gone off with the owner to have a brew. They were talking and enjoying the two cans of beer each, which had been waiting for them when they arrived. True to his word, the screw had not gone into the tack room and had left them on their own while he went back to the house for his drink. John suspected however it may have been for something a little bit stronger than tea.

Mr Gregson arrived about an hour later and walked into the tack room to notice all the empty cans in the box in which they had arrived. "Right boys, let's get back home, looks like the stable boys had a bit of a party last night," he said smiling and looking at the box of cans.

"Sure does," John replied returning his smile and noticing a little glow on the screw's face. "Enjoy your cup of tea?" John asked with a knowing look on his face.

It was ten thirty after night-time inspection and the gang of four were once more sitting around John's bed talking, and the question of Christmas arose which was not far away. They all went into a state of silence, thinking about their loved ones at home over the festive season. Festive, John thought, what is going to be festive about this year?

Terry was the first to speak, "This will be the second time in nick over Christmas," he said.

"What's it like?" Brad asked.

"Fucking awful, and I mean awful. Christmas Day is the worst. All the screws are on tenterhooks waiting for something to kick off, which it normally does," Terry replied with a distant look on his face as if he was looking back to time gone by.

John tried to change the subject to that of release dates. "When yours?" he asked Terry.

"Second week of March," he replied.

"That's just a week before me," John said, sorry he had brought the subject up.

Brad and Garry both said at the same time, "Don't even bother to ask me." John was even more sorry now that he had brought up the subject. They all sat around the bed, all of them very quiet, when John suddenly remembered. "Who wants a whiskey?"

"We haven't got any," Brad said with a frown.

Terry looked at John and said, "You didn't?"

John smiled and replied, "Oh yes I did," and went to his work coat at the side of his bed. He picked it up and brought a Tupperware container out of his pocket. Inside was the whiskey from the tack house.

"You clever bastard."

"Aren't I just?" John replied with a huge grin. The atmosphere changed.

The following morning, the snow had started falling quite heavily and they were all sitting around the work hut wondering what work they were to do today, now that the farm work was completed when Mr Gregson came in. "Morning boys," he said with his usual smile. "We have a new job on for the next few weeks that I think you will like."

"Don't tell us it's outside work," John said looking out of the window at the falling snow which by now had turned into a virtual blizzard.

"No," the screw replied. "You will be pleased to know it is all inside work, well nearly all inside work." They were all silent wondering what this NEARLY all inside work was. Gregson started to tell them. "Well all the chairs in the canteen are looking the worse for wear and we have a back up set in the warehouse by the timber yard, so we have to get all the chairs from the canteen and take them over to the warehouse and rub them down and re-paint them."

"There's fucking hundreds of them, it will take for ever," Terry said.

"Yes?" the screw replied, "got anything else to do?"

Half an hour later after a brew in the work hut they were standing outside the warehouse and the screw was opening the large double doors. Inside they were confronted by a massive area filled with all sorts of things including the stacks of chairs that were to be transported over to the canteen to replace the ones to be painted.

Once again Terry said, " Fucking hell, there are hundreds of the bastards."

"Yeh," John replied knocking the snow off his coat, "should last us till summer or at least till March," he winked at Terry, as he pointed outside to the snow which was still falling very heavy.

Terry took his meaning and broke out into a huge smile, "Yeh, get your point," he said.

"Right," Gregson said, "the first thing we must do is to sort out the best way to do this job. I think if two of you go over to the canteen and collect, shall we say the first ten chairs and bring them back over here, and some of you get down to sanding them down while the others do the re-painting, and take the ones we have in storage here that were painted last year over to the canteen to replace the ones being done here. OK, now who wants to collect the chairs from the canteen?"

John looked at Terry and nodded, "We will do that," John said pointing to Terry.

"Right get on with it," the screw replied.

John and Terry made their way out of the warehouse and past the wood shop and timber yard to the canteen. By the time they got there, they were both covered in snow. As they entered Terry turned to John and said, "That was a fucking good idea, volunteering us for this job when the rest are nice and warm indoors."

"Yeh, but have you thought we can control the speed of the work, and we are in the place where there are lots of cups of tea and food." The words were hardly out of his mouth when one of the men who worked in the kitchen came over to them.

"Come for the chairs have you, mate?" he said to John.

"Yep," John replied.

"Want a brew first?" the man asked. John looked at Terry and gave him a told you so wink. They sat down by one of the tables drinking tea and eating some cake that had been left over from the previous day's pudding. They then collected four of the chairs and set off back to the warehouse. When they arrived Gregson was waiting for them.

"Been a long time collecting those," he said pointing to the four chairs.

"Yeh, thing is," John said, "some of the chairs are in perfect condition and don't need re-painting so we thought we would select the worst of them first and then the others can be done if we have time at a later date."

The screw looked at them in turn and replied, "That makes sense. OK get four out of storage and take them back over to the canteen."

Once more they were back in the canteen and sitting down by one of the tables cup of tea in hand. "I wonder how many cups of tea and how much cake the guys have had this morning?" John said with a sarcastic smile on his face.

"OK, OK, now fuck off, point taken," Terry replied.

The day had finished and the usual four were sitting round sharing a joint and discussing what had gone on during the day. Telling Garry about the scam with the chairs and the perk of the tea and cake. "Bloody hell, it looks like you have got a job for the rest of your stay in here," Garry said.

"Yeh, only thing is it's fucking cold on the ears," replied Terry.

The next morning they were back at the warehouse to be met by Mr Gregson sporting a large grin. "Good morning guys," he said to John and Terry. "Got some good news for you."

"What's that?" John asked.

"A truck," he replied. "I have found an old truck at the back of the warehouse, which means you can load about ten chairs at a time, so you don't have to go over to the canteen as many times and you can help with the painting. Plus the fact it means the job can be completed twice as fast." John and Terry just looked at each other; the screw led them to the back of the warehouse and pointed to a rusty old flat-top truck with four equally rusty wheels. "All you have to do is go over to the wood shop and see if they have any oil," the screw said to John.

With that John walked back to the warehouse door and over to the woodwork shop. As he walked in he was met by the screw in charge of joinery unit. He explained why he had come and the screw directed him to a store cupboard at the bottom of the workshop where he could get a tin of oil. As he entered the store cupboard he noticed there were shelves of varnish, saws and everything that would be wanted for the workshop. He found a large tin of oil on one of the shelves and took it down. As he was walking out he noticed a box full of ear protectors and his mind flew back to Terry's words the previous night about the job being good but it was fucking cold on the ears. He looked around to make sure nobody could see him and took two pairs of the protectors out of the box and put them in his jacket pocket.

He arrived back at the warehouse to find Mr Gregson and Terry standing by the rusty old truck. Terry had cleaned it up a bit and was trying to turn one of the wheels that was even more rusty than the rest and hard to turn round. "Ah, got some oil, I see," the screw said to John noticing the large tin under his arm. "Give it to your mate to put on the wheels."

John handed the tin to Terry who removed the top and started to pour it over the metal frame and wheels of the truck. After a few minutes, the wheels were turning round quite freely. Fuck, John thought, hoping the bloody thing was not going to be used. "Well that's going to help and save time," the screw said.

Yeh and that means we lose out on many cups of tea and cake, John thought.

They were walking across the yard towards the warehouse pulling the newly serviced truck with ten chairs on the back when John said, "We have to get rid of this fucking thing, otherwise we will be in the shed painting the bastard chairs and miss out on our half hour rest period and all that tea and grub."

"Yeh," Terry replied, "but we can't just lose it."

"NO, but it can have a breakdown." They were just passing the wood shop when John had an idea. "Hang on here a minute," he said to Terry. With that walked over to the woodwork shop and went inside. A minute or two later he walked back out with a small lump hammer in his hand.

"What the fuck is that for?" Terry asked.

"Truck maintenance," he replied. They pulled the truck down by the side of the warehouse where they could not be seen and John walked round to the back of the truck. He took the hammer off the top of the truck and gave the back wheel a bloody great crack. Nothing happened. He gave it another blow and the joint of the wheel split and the truck fell on to one side and all the chairs fell off.

"Oops the wheel has fallen off," he said as he looked at Terry with a smile. They picked up two chairs each and walked into the warehouse where Mr Gregson was waiting for them.

"Where's the truck?" he asked with a questioned look on his face.

"Wheel fell off," John replied.

"What do you mean, the wheel fell off?" the screw asked.

"Well we were coming back from the canteen with ten chairs, and I was saying to Terry how good it was to have the truck and not having to carry the chairs when the wheel just fell off."

"Can we repair it?" the screw asked.

"Nope, not a chance, too rusty."

"Well we will just have to go back to carrying them back and forward," Gregson said.

"Yeh, real bastard, going to take us lots more time and we won't be able to sit in the comfort of the warehouse with a paint brush," John replied.

The job carried on for a few weeks and John and Terry were quite happy going back and forth to the canteen each time having tea and cake with the occasional bacon sandwich during the morning, even the problem of the cold ears had been cured with the help of the ear defenders and two pairs of woollen socks.

Chapter 17

Christmas was upon them and the nearer it had come the more the atmosphere in the prison deteriorated. The guys were all up tight and the smallest thing caused at best a slinging match with the occasional punch thrown. Christmas Eve and all the guys were lying on their beds, even the gang of four were not around John's bed but were lying on their own beds staring into space, each one thinking of their loved ones knowing that they would be spending Christmas alone or at least without their husbands and boyfriends. It was at this point that John realised that the punishment of imprisonment was nothing compared to the punishment that he and his fellow prisoners had imposed on their families. If ever there was an incentive not to re offend this was the time, John thought. If ever he was capable of writing a book about his experiences in prison that the reader would laugh at the funny side but more important they would take to heart the hurt he felt now, not for himself but for his wife and children.

Christmas Day and the gang of four walked down to the canteen for their dinner. They walked in comparative silence only now and again putting in the odd word of forced humour. The meal was fantastic with all the things you would expect from a home cooked Christmas dinner. However, at times during the meal, John found it hard to eat as his mind went back to Amy and the children wondering if they were sitting down at the table and what the children's faces were like when they opened their presents.

It was back to work again and they continued with re-painting the chairs, until one afternoon a few weeks later John realised they were almost finished. "Fuck me," he said to Terry, "looks like our playtime is coming to an end, there is only about one more day's work."

"Well it looks like it's back to the bloody fields and working in the cold again," Terry replied.

John looked deep in thought, and then looked at Terry with that impish grin on his face. "Maybe not," he said to his partner in crime. "Look how long does the screw spend in the warehouse each day?" Terry looked at him knowing he had some scheme on his mind.

"Well first thing in the morning, then just before lunch and then just before we finish for the day, why?"

"Well all the chairs we have been working on over the past few weeks are now in storage, and by now the first lot will be dry. How about if we took the chairs that we have brought over here from storage goes back for re-painting and we bring the ones we have just painted back to the canteen?"

Terry just looked at him. "You're crazy," he said to John. "That way it could go on for fucking years."

"We don't want years," John replied, "we only want weeks until we are both out of here."

Terry said, "Why not? Let's do it."

This went on for a week or two until one night when they were all in the canteen having their evening meal. They had just finished when they noticed an inmate get up from the table next to theirs. As he stood up and turned to take his plate back, John noticed he had a broad green stripe along his back and all over his arse. Terry and John looked at each other in disbelief.

"Fucking hell we must have got a chair mixed up and brought over a newly painted one."

As the man started walking out of the canteen a screw stopped him and started talking to him before letting him leave the canteen. The screw walked over to where the man had been sitting and examined the chair. He picked it up and removed it to the back of the room.

"How the fuck did we get them mixed up?" Terry said.

John thought for a moment and then turned to him. "The only thing I can think is that when we got one of the newly painted chairs from storage we must have got one that had only just been painted.

"Oh fuck," they both said together.

The following morning they were on their way to the warehouse when they saw Mr Gregson and a senior screw going into the canteen. About fifteen minutes later Mr Gregson came into the warehouse carrying the chair. He looked at John and said, "Can you please explain what happened here?"

"Must have got mixed up," John replied.

"Mixed up? Mixed up? How the fuck can they have got mixed up?" It was the first time they had heard the screw swear. "All the newly painted chairs are put over there, and all the stored chairs are piled up over there." Pointing to the other end of the room, "so how the fuck did they get mixed up?" This time he directed the question to Terry.

"Don't know," Terry replied.

"Sure it wasn't some kind of practical joke?" he asked.

"No sir," John said.

"Well it doesn't matter now because my boss thinks enough time has been spent on this job and has instructed me to pull everyone off it. We will finish today and tomorrow you will report back to the work hut."

They all sat around John's bed that night sharing a coke bottle half full of whiskey that Garry had obtained.

They had told Garry about the chair escapade and he just smiled at John, "This is one of your tricks isn't it?" he said to John.

"Is it fuck," he replied.

"OK, OK, I will believe you," sounding none too convincing. They shared the bottle round until just after midnight and talked about the pending release of Terry and John.

"I want to tell you all something before I go to bed." Terry said. They all looked at him.

"What's that?" Garry said.

"I don't want to go out of here fucking blue."

John laughed, and said, "No, we will not let you go out blue."

"Thank you," Terry said with a smile as he got up to go to his own bed.

"We were thinking more of a deep red," Brad said as Terry was walking away. All of them laughed apart from Terry, who turned round and gave them all the finger.

They stood in the doorway of the canteen after breakfast looking at the pouring rain. "What a bloody day to go back to outside work," John said. They walked down the yard towards the work hut and by the time they arrived they were all soaking wet.

Mr Gregson was waiting for them inside the hut. "Well boys, looking forward to working outside today?" he said with a grin.

"You must be joking," Terry said.

"Well I have some good news for you, one of the jobs for our little team in the future was waxing the gym floor. As I say for the future. I have had a word with Davd Mackinskey, the officer in charge, and he has agreed to bring it forward for you to start today in view of the lousy weather. So you lucky boys can keep nice and dry for the next two days. Note, I said TWO days that means you do not spin it out for a week by going over it twice because you did half a job the first time. Oh, by the way you two," looking at John and Terry, "you made a good job of keeping the work going with the re-painting of the chairs," he said with a knowing look on his face. John realised that the screw knew the scam they had pulled. "I understand that you," pointing to Terry, "are out next week and you," pointing to John, "are out the week after."

"Yes sir," they both said together.

"Well I will keep your jobs open for you here, for when you come back."

"That's not funny," John said, "you can let mine go, because there is no way you will see me back in here."

"Good," The screw said. "What about you?" looking at Terry. "Do I keep your job over?"

"No thanks Mr Gregson I'm with John. No way I will commit another crime to end up back here."

"Let's hope you haven't anything outstanding from before you came in here," he said. Both John and Terry knew exactly what he was implying, the greatest fear of every inmate on his release from prison.

They arrived at the gym to be met by David Makinskey. "Morning guys," he said as they walked in. "Come with me I'll show you where all the cleaning materials and wax are kept."

They walked across the gym to a large cupboard at the bottom. They entered to find rows of brushes, mops and tins of cleaning materials. "Right guys, the brushes are for sweeping the floors before you apply the wax with those mops over there and those big fluffy mops are to polish, OK? What I would suggest you do is to decide who is to do what. I'm sure I can leave you all to sort that out between you. Right carry on and I will pop back later to see how you are doing." With that he turned and started walking back down the gym to his office.

As soon as he was out of sight John grabbed hold of three of the large brushes kept one himself and gave the other two to Terry and Brad. He had decided it was easier to brush the floor rather than applying the wax and polishing. None of the others bothered to question his decision.

By morning break time they had swept about half the floor area and the others had started to apply the wax. They all went to the small room in the gym annex to make themselves a brew and then went back to the gym to sit on the benches, which ran the full length of one side of the room. They had finished their tea when John noticed four badminton rackets and two shuttlecocks in the corner. "Fancy a knock about for ten minutes?" John asked the guys. There was still one of the nets left up at the bottom of the gym.

"Why not," Terry, Brad and one of the other men said. The four of them got up and went over to collect the badminton equipment and took it over to the net.

"Due to the fact that we only have fifteen minutes left, I suggest we play doubles," John said.

Terry said, "Does anybody know the rules?"

Brad said, "Well I have played a few times," and started to explain how the game was played and how to score. John teamed up with Brad and Terry with the other man. They had been playing for about ten minutes and it seemed they had taken to the game quite quickly, when Brad was in front of John and whipped his hand back to return a high shot. CRACK, Brad's racket connected with the bridge of John's nose.

John dropped to his knees with blood pouring from the cut on his nose. "Fuck me," he said, still on his knees. Just then the gym screw came in and noticed John who had stood up by then with blood down his face. He came over to John and asked Brad what had happened. Brad explained as the screw took John's hand away from his face to inspect the injury.

"Oh dear," David Makinskey said, "that's a good one, better get over to the medic centre and let the doc have a look at that." He got a towel off one of the hooks on the wall; he handed the towel to John and instructed him to press it hard on the bridge of his nose.

John sat on the chair outside the doctor's office waiting to be seen. After five minutes of waiting the door opened and a man in a white coat indicated for him to come in. "Sit down," the man said pointing to a chair in front of his desk. He came over and took the towel off John's face. "That needs a stitch or two. What's your job here?" he asked John.

"Grounds," John replied.

"And your officer?"

"Mr Gregson," he again replied. The doctor went over to a radio station and spoke into it.

"Hello Mr Gregson, I have one of your lads here with a split nose which needs hospital treatment, are you free to come over?" There was a moment's silence and a voice from the other side replied, "Yes, OK, will be over in five minutes."

Ten minutes later they were driving through the prison gates with Mr Gregson in the driving seat and John at the side of him. "Do you mind answering a question?" the screw asked.

"What's that?" John replied.

"What were you doing playing badminton while you were working?"

"Wasn't working, we were on our morning break."

"Ah, that's OK then, just thought I would check."

Some fifteen minutes later they were walking towards the A&E department of the hospital and up to the reception desk. The screw spoke to the receptionist behind the desk who by now had received a call from the doctor at the nick. The receptionist said that John would be seen to next and directed them to a waiting room. As they entered John noticed there were about seven people sitting on chairs waiting to receive treatment. They sat down and all eyes from people waiting turned to look at them. It was not surprising as John knew he must have stood out like a sore thumb, him in full prison uniform and a screw in full uniform at the side of him. I wonder if they have guessed that I am a prisoner; he smiled to himself knowing all to well what they thought. He thought at one time if he should growl and look a bit demented to confirm that he was a criminal under guard and then thought better of it.

The doctor came out from behind a curtain and looked at his escort and asked them to come forward. They stood up and walked to the curtain area where the doctor asked John to sit down on a metal chair. John did as he was told and the white-coated man came over to him. The doctor looked at John's nose and said, "That's a good cut, but I think we will get away with just the one stitch." By now John's left eye was starting to close a little. Ten minutes and one stitch later they were walking out of the A&E department to the gaze of all the people in the area.

They arrived back at the nick about an hour after they had left and Gregson, as instructed by the doctor, told John to go back to the dorm and lie down. He lay on his bed and the next thing he knew the lads were around his bed.

"How are you?" Terry asked.

"OK, feel fine," John replied, looking at him through one eye, the other by now had almost closed.

"Sorry about that," Brad said.

"No problem," John replied, "but who won the game?"

"Well up to me decking you, we were in front," Brad said. John looked at Terry and made an L out of his index finger and thumb and at the same time chanted, "LOSER, LOSER." The guys just laughed.

The following morning over breakfast they all asked John how he was. "Not well, got a fucking bad headache," he said to them. "I don't think I am fit for work today," with a wink to Brad. "I think you have been paid by that bastard," pointing to Terry to get revenge.

Terry having a good grasp of the English language just said, "Fuck off."

The lads went off to work back at the gym and John went over to the medical block to report sick. As he entered the doctor was standing in the waiting room. "Good morning, Davidson," the doctor said, "and how are you feeling?"

"OK," John replied. "Apart from a blinding headache."

"Well, the best thing you can do is go back to your dorm and lay on your bed and rest. Where are you working at the moment?"

"Over at the gym," John replied.

"OK," the doctor said. "I will contact the officer there and inform him that you will not be working today."

"Thank you," said John, as he turned and walked out of the medical unit and returned to the dorm. It was a quiet day, lying on his bed and thinking only a short while now and he would be back with his loved ones.

The guys came back from work having completed the work in the gym and that night sat around John's bed having a smoke and talking about Terry getting out in two days' time and John the following week. The other two guys didn't seem to join in the excitement. Not surprising, John thought, when they still had over a year before they were looking forward to walking out of the prison gates. John thought it was a good idea to change the subject for the sake of Brad and Garry.

Morning once more came and once again it was raining like hell. John wondered if he could get away swinging it for another day off work but decided he would be pushing it too much so he and the other two set off across the yard towards the work hut. Once more, by the time they arrived, they were soaked to the skin. John had thought sometime ago why all the waterproof clothing had to be left in the work hut and could not be taken back to the dorm. It was only when Terry had told him that at one time they could bring them back until some of the men were selling them at the perimeter wall after lights out. So they put a stop to it.

Mr Gregson arrived at the hut a few minutes after them, and with his usual smile said. "Nice day again, boys."

"Yeh," they all replied, thinking about the next eight hours out in the rain.

"Right got some good news for you, you will be pleased to know that you will not be working in the rain today, due to the fact that a wagon full of wood is arriving at the wood shop in about half an hour's time and it has to be unloaded and put in stores." All of them looked at the screw with beaming smiles on their faces.

"Nice one," Terry said.

As they arrived at the wood store the wagon was just turning in. One of the lads who worked there was opening the huge store door and started to wave the wagon to reverse into the unit. When it was eventually parked up, Mr Gregson came over to them. "Right lads, I want all the timber taken off the wagon and put in the timber racks over there," he ordered, pointing to rows of metal cages. "Now I am sure you will realise that this is not going to take all day if you work fast, so all I will say is that as soon as you have finished you are all working in the fields, outside in the rain, so I would prefer a good neat job even if it means taking a little longer," he said with a wink.

Brad looked at him and said, "You do know that if we stack it perfect it could take all day!"

"You catch on quick my son," the screw replied.

It was at this point that a half-caste guy walked into the unit escorted by a screw that John had not seen before. "Can you give this man some work just for today. He gets out tomorrow and has been working in the laundry room, and all the guys in there are refusing to work with him. He is causing trouble over there. He has lost all his remission and feels he can do what he wants," the screw said. The half-caste guy just smiled at the screw.

"OK, leave him with me, I am sure my guys will help him," Gregson replied.

"Don't want any help, 'cos I'm doing fuck all and there is nothing you can fucking do about it," the half-caste replied.

John and Terry looked at each other. John thinking, no but we can.

"Right lads, I want two of you on the wagon to pass the wood down, and the rest of you to stack the timber in the racks." John and Terry jumped up on to the trailer and the half-caste guy sat down on the floor. "Get up," Mr Gregson said.

"Fuck off," the man on the floor said.

Brad came over to him and said, "Come on, mate, we work as a team here, so why not help us. After all you are out tomorrow, why cause waves?"

"Go fuck yourself," the man replied.

John and Terry looked at each other before they jumped down off the top of the trailer. "I don't think he understands," John said to the screw. "If you have something to do boss, maybe we can talk him into helping us."

Mr Gregson smiled. "OK guys, get on with your work while I go to the office to get the delivery note. I will be about fifteen minutes." The screw walked out of the building and John and Terry walked over to the man sitting on the ground.

John looked down at him and said, "Come on, we have a good screw here who looks after us, so get up and give us a hand."

"Look, I have lost all my time off and I'm out tomorrow and nobody can make me do nothing if I don't want to," he replied. He cried out in pain as Terry gave him a kick in the top of his leg. "You bastard!" he said. "I'll report you for assault when the screw comes back."

Terry gave him an even harder kick this time and said, "Report that as well, now fucking get up and put those gloves on," pointing to a pair of rigger gloves by the side of the wagon.

The man got up and turned to Terry, "You still can't make me do any work."

John gave him one hell of a punch in the kidneys and he dropped to the floor with a gasp of breath. Terry gave him one more kick in the top of his leg.

"OK, OK," the man said. "I'll put the fucking gloves on."

Terry went over and collected the gloves and threw them at him. The man stood up and started to put them on just as Mr Gregson came back into the shed.

"Everything OK?" he said to the men.

"NO everything is not OK," the half-caste said. "Those two bastards have given me a kicking and I want them put on a charge."

"Us?" John replied.

"We haven't touched him," Terry said.

"All the others saw it," the man said looking round the room.

The screw looked round at the other men and said, "Well, who saw the assault on this man?" He looked around to see all the men shaking their heads. "Sorry looks like nobody saw anything," Gregson said.

"OK," the man said, "but you still can't make me do any work."

"Have you got any more paperwork to collect boss?" John asked the screw.

The screw looked at John with a smile. "Well as it so happens I have, it will take me about half an hour."

The half-caste looked at John with a look of trepidation, realising he was about to receive another kicking as soon as the screw left. "OK, OK, I'll do some work."

"Good boy," Terry said with a wink at the screw.

At the end of the day the wagon had been unloaded, with the help of the half-caste even though he had to be reminded now and again with the odd slap from John and Terry.

They were sitting back in the dorm and asking Terry what he was going to do when he got out the day after tomorrow.

"The first thing is to take my wife out to the local as soon as they open and then get my feet up at home ready for an early night," he smiled. "One thing I am going to do right now though, is have a shower before tomorrow night as I don't trust you bastards on my last night." With that he got up to collect his towel from his locker.

"What are we going to do?" Garry asked. "There is no way he is going to leave the dorm tomorrow night and even if he did, suspending his bed from the ceiling is out and now he has had a shower we can't even send him on his way a pretty colour."

"Just have to play it as it comes," John replied.

Chapter 18

The following night, prior to Terry's release in the morning, they were all sitting around talking when John had a good idea. "Anyone fancy a brew?" John asked.

"Yeh," they all agreed.

"Could you do the honours while I roll a couple of joints?" John asked Terry, handing him his cup.

Terry took it but looked a bit suspicious. "What the fuck are you up to?" he said to John, fully aware that they would try and find some way to get to him.

"Nothing," John replied.

"If you think we are planning anything, forget it, we have decided that you have covered everything and you can leave with nothing but a fond farewell."

"OK," Terry said, "but I want you to help me with the tea. I still do not trust you out of my sight."

"Fine," John replied. "Come on, let's go." They both stood up and started walking down the dorm towards the boiler room. As they got there Terry pushed the door open and walked inside with the four cups, he had not noticed the brush at the side of the door. As he started pouring the boiling water into the cups, John slowly walked back out of the room and took hold of the long brush. He pulled the door shut on Terry and put the handle of the brush through the handle of the door making it impossible for Terry to open the door from the inside.

Terry realised he had been caught and there was nothing he could do about it.

Garry and Brad arrived at the boiler room door to hear Terry's voice from inside shouting, "Let me out you bastards!"

"Now what are we going to do?" Brad asked.

John said, "Come on you two," as he walked over to Terry's bed. "Get it to the fire doors, we are going to put it on the island on the lake." After a great deal of effort, the bed had been carried across the field, over the bridge and deposited on the island. John looked at it with a look of satisfaction as they retraced their steps back to the dorm.

On entering the dorm John said, "Well I suppose we had better let him out," and with that set off in the direction of the boiler room to hear Terry banging on the door. Garry removed the brush handle and opened the door.

"OK you bastards what have you been up to?" Terry said, with that he looked over to his bed area. "OK, where the fuck is it?" he asked noticing the absence of his bed. John just shrugged his shoulders. Terry went into the washroom thinking they had put his bed in there. He came out and again asked with a smile on his face, "Where the hell have you put it?"

John replied, "Well seeing it is your last night we thought we would give it a bit of an airing so it would be nice and fresh for you."

"An airing? What the fuck do you mean an airing?"

John walked towards the fire doors as they all followed him. When they got there John pointed out over the field towards the lake. Terry followed John's gaze over the field and to the island in the middle of the lake. "What the... how am I going to get it back from there?" Knowing the rule of no help on the last night. "Come on guys, you have got to give me a hand with this one."

"Sorry," Garry said as he walked away. "Got some education work to do before morning."

"And I have pulled my back," John said smiling as he held his back and lay down on his bed.

"Sorry I would have given you a lift, but John has threatened to give me a good kicking if I do, and I know you would not like that to happen to me," Brad said.

"You bastards," Terry said as he went out of the fire door and set off in the direction of the lake.

Two hours later Terry was outside the fire doors again with sweat pouring out of him even though it was a very cold night.

John got up off his bed and went over to the doors and opened them. "Come on mate," he said, "let me give you a hand, I'll hold the doors open for you."

Terry just looked at him and replied, "Thanks a fucking bundle," as he dragged his bed through the doors.

John said with a smile, "Oh by the way Terry, did you make the tea while you were in the boiler room?" Terry just looked at him.

Fifteen minutes later the four of them were sitting around John's bed drinking the tea they should have had almost three hours ago. This time Garry had made it as they thought they could not shame Terry by asking him to make it.

Terry looked at John and said, "I'm not even going to ask whose idea that little prank was, but I promise I will pay you back for it you bastard." It was said with a smile as Terry knew there was nothing nasty in the act, and deep down found it nice that they had taken the interest and time to pull it off.

"You will have to be quick," John replied. "You only have about eight hours left in this dump." They sat around until about midnight when Terry decided it was time to go to bed and get some sleep before his six o'clock rise and freedom. They all shook Terry's hand and wished him all the luck in the world.

The following morning when they awoke they all looked down at Terry's bed and noticed it was stripped and all his things had gone off his locker. Garry and Brad came over to John and said, "Well that lucky bastard will probably be having his breakfast at home with his family."

"Yeh, but he still not get back at me for the bed prank," he said with a smile.

Chapter 19

Time went very slowly for John during the next week. He could not concentrate on anything apart from the fact that within the next few days he would be home with his darling wife and children, and of course the chance to re-join his company in a new job. During the week nothing happened apart from the general day-to-day work. There was no more fun – that seemed to have walked out of the prison with Terry. He reflected how he had come to be so friendly with the man after such a bizarre start outside the post room.

John had just finished his last day's work and had his last meal in the canteen and was sitting on his bed contemplating his release the following morning, when Garry and Brad came over to him and sat on the chairs by his bed. John looked up at them and said, "Before we go any further, I don't want a game of snooker, I don't want to watch any television, I am not going to have a shower and I will not go and make a brew, OK?" They both looked at him and smiled.

"That's OK," Garry said, "you just lie on your bed to protect it."

"GOT IT ONE," John replied with a grin on his face. It was about nine o'clock when John noticed Garry and Brad talking to some other guys at the bottom of the dorm. Suddenly about ten of them, including Garry and Brad, turned and started to walk up the dorm to John's bed. Oh fuck! John thought, this is it. His first thought was to make a break for it out of the fire door, then realised he would be leaving his bed unattended and it was after nine o'clock lock up.

He got up off his bed and put his back against the wall, as the men got within ten feet of him John said, "I'm fucking warning you, the first person to touch me I will drop him." Knowing all too well he could not carry out his threat.

They all grabbed him at once and sat him on one of the chairs by his bed. One of the men produced a roll of plastic coated duck tape out of his pocket and within five minutes John was taped firmly to the metal chair. All the men stood back with a look of satisfaction on their faces.

"OK, very funny," John said, "how long do you expect me to be tied up like this?"

"Oh we haven't finished yet," Garry said reaching into John's locker taking out a selection of broad felt tip pens.

"Oh no," John said.

"Oh yes," Brad replied. Within a short while John had been made up with deep red lips, blue cheeks and thick black rings round his eyes. They then carried him to the corridor which was by this time out of bounds. After putting him outside they all retreated back in the dorm to await the arrival of the night screw for his dorm inspection.

Ten o'clock on the dot, the screw arrived at the entrance to the dorm. When he saw John he just stopped and looked at him, said nothing and just came in the dorm and continued his inspection as if nothing was out of the norm. After about half an hour he had completed his walk round the dorm and was just about to leave when he walked up to John, smiled, and then turned back to the men in the dorm.

"Get him back in now, before one of my less lenient friends see him." He walked away just shaking his head.

It was midnight and John was still tied to the chair, which by this time, had been put on top of the large table in the middle of the dorm.

"Will you wankers get me down from here, I'm dying for a pee," John shouted. Garry and one of the lads came over to him.

"Can you hang on until about five?" Garry said.

"NO, I fucking well can't hang on till five," John replied, feeling a little desperate.

"What do you think?" Garry said to the other man.

"Well, it's us that will have to clean the floor, so go on cut him down."

They were sitting down around John's bed having a brew when he was eventually released from the chair. "You bastards," he said. "That was a bit over the top." Not being able to suppress a smile, "I had better get all this stuff off my face before morning," and with that collected his soap and towel from his locker and headed off to the shower room. He came back about fifteen minutes later to be met with peels of laughter from the guys who were still up. He got back to his bed to find Garry and Brad in tears of laughter as well. He had managed to wash most of the felt tip off his face as it was water based but the black around his eyes had been a spirit base and he could only get a small amount off and had distributed most it in a circle around his eyes.

Garry had tears running down his face with laughter, "You look like a fucking panda," he said laughing even more now.

Eventually they finished their tea and the last joint and John said his goodbyes to them, after shaking hands with them both and the two men wishing John all the best for the future, Garry and Brad went back to their own beds.

John tried to sleep when he got in bed but found that he was far too excited at his pending freedom and could only drop off for short periods of time, waiting for six o'clock to arrive and for him to gather all his things and go to the release reception area.

Five thirty arrived and he could stand it no longer. He got out of bed and got dressed; half an hour later he was walking down the corridor with all his bedding and his possessions in pillowcases. When he arrived at the reception, the lights were on, and he walked in to be confronted by one of the screws. He gave him his name and number, and the screw picked up a sheet of paper off his desk. Looking down at this, and without looking up at John, he just said, "Right Davidson, strip." He did as he was told while the man went into another room and brought out some boxes and clothes on hangers covered by polythene bags. The screw put them down on the table in front of him and told him to get dressed.

John noticed that his clothes had all been cleaned and ironed – even his shoes had a high polish. When he had finished the screw looked at him and asked where he was going after his release. John told him he was going to his home, and the screw read out his address and asked John if that was correct. He confirmed that it was and the screw handed him an envelope which he instructed him to open and check the contents. Inside he found money and took it out.

"Count it," the screw said. He did as he was instructed. "How much?" the screw asked.

"Thirty-five pounds," John replied.

The man pushed a piece of paper over to him, "Sign that to say that you have received it." John again did as he was instructed. The screw looked at the clock on the wall. "Five to seven, you can go in five minutes, Davidson." With that he left him and went into another room. Five minutes seemed like an hour but then he was walking towards the gatehouse and freedom.

He felt ten feet tall and was smiling to himself – a few hours more and he would be with his family again never ever to be parted again.

He walked through the gates and towards the road to set off on his walk to the bus stop when he noticed two tall men in dark suits step out in front of him. One of the men was holding up what appeared to be a card. "John Davidson?" the man asked in rather a stern way.

John replied, "Yes, that's me."

"I have a warrant for your arrest," the man said.

John's head exploded. He could feel himself shouting in silence, NO, NO. He felt he was going to be sick; it was then he noticed another man step out of the shadows.

John could not see too well but soon recognised the voice of Terry when he said, "Told you I would get you back you bastard." Terry walked up to him with his hand held out sporting a huge grin. "These two guys are friends of mine. Come on, jump in the car, let's take you home."